HaHa! Britain

Written by 40 Chinese authors
Translated by 37 volunteer translators

A literature project conceived by

PROPOLINGO PUBLISHING LTD

PROPOLINGO

English Copyright © The Mothers' Bridge of Love

"The Big Ben" on Cover: Feng Tang
Cover Calligraphy: Qu Leilei
Cover Design and Illustrations: Tian Tian
Editor: Yang Yang

All rights reserved. No part of this publication may be reproduced, stored or introduced into a retrieval system, or transmitted, in any form or by any means (electronic, mechanical, photocopying, recording or otherwise) without the prior written permission of the publisher except for the use of quotation in a book review.

ISBN: 978-1-9136460-0-4

A CIP catalogue recorded for this book is available from the British Library.

First Published in Great Britain in 2024 by

Propolingo Publishing Ltd.

5 Kew Road, Richmond, London, TW9 2PR

www.propolingo.com

Printed & Bound in China

In 1687, a lone Chinese man set sail,
Across oceans wide, to the British Isles.
Three centuries hence, brilliant events unveiled,
Four hundred thousand roots in foreign soil.
Yet, away from Nine sacred realms they dwelled,
Homesick and estranged, the Yellow Emperor's kin.
Modest and reserved, their nature held,
Jet-black eyes countless, yet unseen within.
Let alone the endeavours, to make Chinese voices heard,
To their posterity, like candlelight, flickering in the night.

Small though it may seem,
When gathered, candlelights could set the land ablaze,
With determination and hope unshackled,
A band of Chinese started a sacred blaze.
As Spring banished Winter's cold embrace,
In the year 2023, with ink and paper,
They spoke unto their kin:
"Write of this foreign land,
And we shall etch your words in the press."
The roar of words, the clink of printing press:
"Hear ye! The pioneering Chinese publication
In Britannia's embrace!"

Over high barriers of different tongues,
Voices traverse with determined will.
English version now prepared,
With a joyful name *HaHa! Britain*,
As Chinese books meet the sun.
Suddenly silent Chinese find their voice,
Across the nation, to British ears,
Their happiness and sorrows converse.

A noble act of charity unfolds in this publication,
Soothing the ache of solitude,
It opens a window to British understanding,
Fertile is the land of Chinese literacy on these isles.
Come, our kin, your pens are ploughs,
Cultivating this envisioned land.

Come, and flip through the leaves,
Roaring, the collective voices of Chinese,
Near and far, beyond the seven seas,
Their resonance firmly seizes your heart.

Editors from The Mothers' Bridge of Love & River Cam Breeze
July 2024

To all the Chinese
who have lived on these islands
over the past four centuries,
and to the British who have truly been their friends.

In a foreign land,
spring colours grow around me;
Moved from my homeland,
I understand the heart of a guest.

Du Fu
Three Poems of Joy Sent to My Younger Brother on His Journey to Fetch His Wife and Children from Lantian to Jiangling - II

Preface

To Be, Or Not To Be?

Written by: Xue Xinran
Translated by: Zhang Heruijie

Whenever I think about sharing my experiences of living and working in the UK for nearly thirty years, my thoughts become a tangled mess. It's difficult to condense so many years – my memories feel like a chaotic landscape of vast skies, clouds, rain, thunder and lightning. Given the limited space, I'll just share a few brief cultural anecdotes.

Because my parents were educated in both English and Russian, I grew up in awe of foreign languages, always fearing I might become their "ignorant offspring". However, fate, guided by Murphy's Law, had other plans – the more you dread something, the more likely it is to happen! In university, English was my worst subject, and I never scored more than 60.5 points out of 100. I vowed never to associate myself with English for as long as I lived.

Yet, as if under Murphy's curse, I found myself "abandoning the light for the dark" and moving to the UK, where I have now spent over twenty years trying to make a living in an English-speaking world. To add to the irony, I was drawn into a traditional English family by love so deep that even my sleep-talking is in English. I often dream about translating Shakespeare's famous line, "To be, or not to be, that is the question", from English into Chinese, as though it were an unending assignment. I still remember how over forty students in one of my classes produced different Chinese translations of that line. When we awaited the standard answer, our famously rigorous teacher surprised us by saying that there is no standard answer for this sentence!

To be, or not to be, that is the question. This sentence has become a shadow accompanying me in a foreign land. This shadow does not follow behind me but leads the way ahead, guiding my path. This is because the light of my life comes from my homeland, family, experiences, knowledge, and the Chinese culture deeply rooted inside me.

I come from a culture that places great emphasis on etiquette, and I've always believed in the importance of the saying, "When in Rome, do as the Romans do" before going abroad. However, the first challenge I encountered in the West was navigating the complexity of greeting customs. In China, men and women traditionally avoid physical contact, and even the practice of shaking hands is a relatively recent development, not much older than a century.

When I arrived in the UK, shaking hands felt straightforward enough, and even the Western custom of men and women hugging became something I got used to over time. Yet, after living and working in the West for more than two full cycles of the Chinese zodiac, I still haven't mastered the art of cheek-kissing in different countries. I understand that for a woman, a man offering a cheek kiss is often a gesture of respect. But do you start from left to right, or right to left? How many times are appropriate?

Sometimes, assuming the person is British, I stop after a hug and a kiss on each cheek. Then, when they offer their cheek for a third time, I realise they are from a different country. If I'm quick to notice, I can respond in time. If not, they've already withdrawn politely while I'm still on tiptoe, craning my neck for a belated kiss. And if they then come back for more, our attempt at a polite greeting suddenly resembles a cha-cha.

Knowing that I am confused about Western greeting customs, my British husband, who considered himself well-travelled, would comfort me by saying, "With more exposure and experience, you'll be able to judge people's greeting culture because their gestures and actions reflect their cultural background."

However, during our travels, I often found my husband apologising for his "incorrect" cheek-kissing. "I forgot this is their territory," he would say. It seems that even cheek-kissing requires adapting to local customs. So now, whenever I prepare for a lecture or attend a conference in a European country, I always double-check the local greeting etiquette with friends.

In my personal experience, greeting etiquette with French people is particularly challenging. Depending on the region of France they come from, the number of cheek kisses varies, typically ranging from one to four times. Moreover, there's variation in whether to start with the left cheek or the right cheek. Parisians begin with the left side, kissing once on each cheek, totalling two kisses. In some regions of Southern France, they start with the right side, resulting in three kisses.

For Spain and Portugal, it's customary to start with the right cheek. In Italy and Greece, it starts with the left cheek, with two kisses. It's said that in Eastern European countries, greetings usually involve two or three kisses. All I can say is, good luck!

As I write this, I recall an incident from twenty years ago when I was teaching part-time at the School of Oriental and African Studies at the University of London. A British male student learning Chinese asked me why Chinese girls are so easily moved, to the point that a hug can make them "surge with emotion". Little did he know that many Chinese girls at that time had never been hugged by anyone, not even their family members. Likewise, in early 2003, during an interview with an Italian female journalist, she remarked that greeting Chinese men felt like facing a stern bronze statue – they were impossible to embrace, nor able to. Perhaps this stems from the fact that Chinese men, raised with a strong sense of modesty and reserve, struggle to respond to the passionate and exuberant greetings of Italian women.

Adapting to British customs feels like an endless journey, not only in terms of language, traditions and rituals, but also in navigating the laws and regulations, which can often be daunting and frustrating. The UK is a society that has evolved over 800 years, shaped by the Magna Carta. The British people's sense of conscientiousness and self-discipline is both admirable and, at times, astonishing to many Chinese, myself included. We are often left perplexed by what can appear to be their "obsessive" adherence to rules.

Once, I saw a new light bulb and £10 on the table at home. When I asked my husband, Toby, about it, he explained that the lamp's lightbulb had burned out, and the money was for a new bulb and the electrician's fee. I was shocked and said, "We can change it ourselves!" Toby responded seriously, "We shouldn't touch anything electric without the proper certification." Flabbergasted, I changed the bulb myself, and kept the fee!

My confusion extends beyond household matters. I have published or co-published more than ten non-fiction books in the UK. Each book goes through five editorial stages: structure, language, typesetting, historical verification and cover design. Every editor would pose questions that left me dumbfounded, such as, "Does everyone in China use chopsticks to eat?" or "Why do you ask about the health of others? Those are private matters!" Or "How can you give someone healthcare products without a medical certification? That's illegal."

For my book *China Witness*, the historical verification editor, a chief editor at Random House, gave me a list of 108 questions, most of which were "unacceptable in English culture". These included, "Why do you point out that someone looks unwell and assume that they are too tired?"

I asked her, "If I visit you in the hospital, can't I ask about your condition?" She replied, "Even if I were dying, I'd expect you to compliment my spirit or appearance. That's how we show politeness and respect in our culture."

Only after her explanation did I understand why Toby often felt hurt by my Chinese friends. "Why are your Chinese friends so worked up about my illness and asking so many questions?" I initially thought it was just his private personality.

Friends in international marriages, like me, experience even more cultural clashes. These can range from amusing misunderstandings to serious family conflicts. Who should adapt to whom? That is the question! At public events I attend, Westerners in international marriages often seek my help in persuading their partners not to force them to eat "Chinese delicacies" that look and sound terrifying to them: stomach, kidneys, brains, hooves, paws, tongues, ears and the like.

When I try to follow through on these requests, my Chinese compatriots often feel deeply aggrieved, "Isn't it all for their benefit?! Don't they know the profound principles of Chinese health preservation? How can they love China without understanding the concept of 'You are what you eat'?"

Fortunately, my husband Toby had a rare "Chinese stomach" for a Brit. He could handle the exotic seafood that scares many Westerners. However, he still couldn't tolerate chicken's feet and congee. His reasoning was that the bones in chicken feet pose a challenge – how can you spit them out after putting them in your mouth without disturbing others' appetites or sensibilities? As for congee, he finds the sound made while eating it reminiscent of pigs grunting, which he considers rather embarrassing.

I remember when I was first allowed to join the adults' dinner table, my grandmother began instructing me on Chinese dining etiquette and taboos: never stick chopsticks upright in the rice bowl, wait for elders to start eating before picking up your chopsticks, use your left hand to support the bowl as a sign of respect for the food, pick the dishes closest to you... and eat without making noise or clattering with chopsticks and spoons on the bowl.

However, these Chinese table manners are difficult to uphold with Western utensils at a Western dining table. Even now, I can't manage to use a knife and fork to debone fish or dissect chicken wings. Shortly after marrying Toby, during a lunch, he affectionately said to me, "Darling, you're so cute, protecting your plates and dishes like British children."

There's an old Chinese saying, "The sound of the gong and drums can speak for the secrets." So I asked him for advice and learned that in Western dining, one should not constantly hold onto the plate. As I began to adapt and stopped using my hands to hold plates and dishes, a waiter at a Chinese restaurant in London said, "You should teach your Western husband to hold the plate with his hand. That's our way of eating!"

So, when dining in a Chinese restaurant in the UK, which set of rules – Chinese or Western – should we follow?

Many Chinese people believe that British people do not respect food. From Toby's family and friends, I've learned that they often emphasise presentation over flavour, paying great attention to table arrangements, utensil placements, flowers, candlelight, and the visual appeal of food. In traditional British households, dinner is considered a "special time" of the day, so they take a shower and change clothes (or at least refresh themselves) before enjoying wine and starting the meal.

I was with Toby for over twenty years, and whenever we had dinner at home, he always took a shower and changed clothes before sitting at our table, even when it was just the two of us. He said it was a family tradition, showing respect for food and dining companions. In contrast, having spent years hosting nightly radio programmes in China, I never had the luxury of enjoying leisurely dinners at home. Although I now live in Toby's country and experience his "British home dining culture", I have yet to fully integrate into this refined English style.

In my twenty years of charity work with The Mothers' Bridge of Love, I often see the confusion of Chinese children growing up in the West. They navigate daily between their Chinese home life and the Western world outside, facing a cultural sandwich of "To be, or not to be". The differences between Chinese and Western cultures are vast – from conflicting beliefs and systems to small customs like whether a sneeze should be quietly endured or openly released. Blowing one's nose: should it be discreet or boldly symphonic?

When dining with others, should the Chinese adhere to Western etiquette by refraining from serving food to others, or should they act in accordance with traditional Chinese customs by serving guests food and rice? In British schools, toilet paper must be flushed down the toilet, but in Chinese restaurants, it must be disposed of in a bin (a source of confusion for friends from many countries, who worry about making the excrement visible to all).

I once met a mixed-race girl in London's Chinatown who refused to use the restroom because there was a magpie in the sink, which she considered unlucky. Her Chinese mother tried to explain that magpies are auspicious birds in Chinese culture. The girl countered, saying she learned in kindergarten: "one for sorrow, two for joy" – indeed, in British culture, seeing one magpie is considered unlucky, while seeing two is fortunate.

It's important to recognise that the concept of "British people" is diverse and multifaceted. Did you know that, according to data from the British government in June 2022, around 14% of the UK population holds British nationality but was born outside the UK? This means that the people we meet every day might not be native-born Britons, and the cultures they represent can add a delightful, if not sometimes comical or confusing twist to traditional British customs. With such a vibrant mix, it's no surprise that for many overseas Chinese, the existential question of "to be, or not to be" resonates deeply in their daily lives as they navigate this colourful and ever-evolving tapestry of cultural exchange.

About the author

Xue Xinran, pen name Xinran, is a British-Chinese journalist, author and volunteer. She began her career in the late 1980s working at a radio station in China and moved to London in 1997, starting from cleaning jobs and later working part-time at the School of Oriental and African Studies, University of London. She began writing *The Good Women of China*, a collection of interview memoirs from her hosting of women's radio programmes like *Words on the Night Breeze*, which was published in 2002 and translated into over 40 languages worldwide. Her other works include *Sky Burial*, *What the Chinese Don't Eat*, *Miss Chopsticks*, *China Witness* and *A Message from an Unknown Chinese Mother*. She has also authored *Buy Me the Sky*, *The Promise/Talking about Love*, *Still Hot*, *The Book of Secrets* and *China Adorned*.

In August 2004, Xinran founded the Mothers' Bridge of Love (MBL) international cultural charity with a group of volunteers, aiming to build bridges between China and the West, adoptive and birth cultures, and poverty and wealth. MBL has long provided counselling and ancestral tracing services for adoptive families of Chinese children worldwide.

The book *Mothers' Bridge of Love*, specially compiled for adoptive families, ranked third on the *Washington Post*'s top 10 children's bestseller list in 2007. By the end of 2021, MBL had helped build 28 rural and urban primary school libraries and, since 2013, has regularly collaborated with the V&A Museum of Childhood in London and China Exchange to host annual Chinese New Year celebrations.

Since March 2020, MBL Multimedia has published 500 *Xinran Essays* to meet the communication needs between overseas students and their families during the COVID-19 isolation period. In February 2021, MBL launched the *Cultural Forum*, an online monthly magazine providing a platform for Sino-Western dialogue to help Chinese people at home and abroad understand the COVID-19 pandemic and support pandemic relief efforts.

Xinran has also served as a cultural consultant for Western media outlets in the UK, USA, and Europe, contributing to current affairs commentary on various television and radio stations. She has served as a literary consultant for the UK's "Asian House" and was named a city hero by *Time Out* magazine's international edition in 2008 as part of its Beijing 40th anniversary celebrations. In 2011, she was recognised as one of the Global Century's 100 Outstanding Women by *The Guardian* in the UK. In 2013, she received an honorary doctorate in anthropology from Hamilton College in the USA. In 2014, *The Good Women of China* was selected by Random House UK as a world literature classic, and *Sky Burial* was included in Penguin's Classic 26 Alphabet series. In 2019, she was named one of the Outstanding Women of the Year in the UK.

Contents

When in Rome...

Don't Touch My Door	5
Are You Alright?	11
Theatre in London: A Must-See Experience	17
"Black Tea, No Milk, Ta"	23
The Taste of Sandwiches	31
My British In-Laws	37
Pants, Underpants and Other Humorous Differences Between British and American English	43
Britain is Old Fashioned, isn't It?	49
My Ten Years in the UK	55
A Green Thumb	61

All Walks of Life

Two Beggars	69
In Memory of Toby Eady	75
Experiencing COVID-19 in the UK	83
A Chance Encounter with Giuseppe Eskenazi	93
My Days in the Plastic Surgery Department	101
Survive or Perish: Learning to Thrive	109
Days of Commuting to an Island by Boat	119
Opening an Art Gallery in London	127

A Kaleidoscope of Faces

Helping You Home 135
A Musical Encounter 143
My Welsh Friend Lloyd 151
My Distant Neighbour Bernice 157
Strangers 163
Like Planes in the Night – a Driving Classical Music *Aficionado* and a Photographer Wearing the Paperboy's Cap 171
Could True Love Be Like This? 177
My British Husband, The Avid Runner 183

Roam in the UK

What is "Posh"? 191
British Accents 197
Right to Roam 203
Sending Letters Home from Red Postboxes 211
My Stories of Edinburgh 217
Birdwatching 225
A Spot of Tea 231
Foodie in London 235
Flower-planting in a Park Sparks Some Thoughts 241
Land of Gardens 249
England to Me 255
Buying Books: Rediscovering Trust in the UK 261
Collecting Second-hand Goods in the UK 269

Afterword

The Vitality of Everyday Life and Cultural Roots 273

Acknowledgements 277

When in Rome...

We know what we are, but know not what we may be.

> William Shakespeare
> *Hamlet*

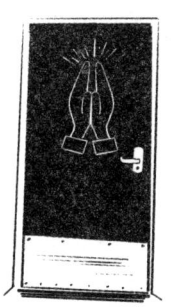

Don't Touch My Door

Written by: Fan Xuequn
Translated by: Yiyang Dong

In the blink of an eye, I have now been teaching Chinese at a secondary school in Cambridgeshire for seven years. It can be said to be both short and long for the development of a discipline. It is short because the time flies, but long because of the numerous changes over the seven years. Seven years ago, we started from scratch when Chinese first became one of our foreign language courses. But now, we not only offer GCSE Chinese courses but have also developed A-level classes. I was all on my own in the beginning, but now I have a teaching team of three Chinese teachers and two teaching assistants. Moreover, the GCSE Chinese exam results have long been outstanding, even becoming one of our school's greatest points of pride.

My teaching career has thus gradually witnessed the rising recognition of Chinese in Cambridgeshire. At first, some students and their parents were doubtful about whether Chinese courses could prosper in an ordinary secondary school in the UK. But after all these years, they not only accept this discipline but also support my unique rules. Among my rules, the most interesting one is "Don't touch my door."

Let's go back to when I first started teaching Chinese. At the time, I had just completed my PGCE at UCL. After an interview, I became the first Chinese teacher at this school and also the first at any public school in Cambridgeshire. As the first East Asian teacher in this school's history, and with only grade seven students learning Chinese, students from other grades were curious about me and the Chinese course. Therefore, they often tried to draw my attention through mischievous acts such as knocking on my door loudly and running away quickly. Sometimes they even added strange noises into the mix, which disrupted my teaching.

Because my classroom is at the corner of the teaching building with a surveillance camera installed in the ceiling, each time an incident like this occurred, I needed to contact the staff to check the CCTV recordings to identify the student responsible. But since students from other grades didn't have Chinese courses, it sometimes took me more than half an hour to finally find the naughty kid.

When I found them, I would bring them to my classroom door, ask them to clasp their hands together and apologize to the door in Chinese saying "dui bu qi", which means "sorry". Although some students found it amusing, they could sense my determination and seriousness in addressing this incident.

This situation continued for about three months, during which the Chinese course was gradually accepted and respected. One day, to test how much respect the seventh-grade students had for me, I asked them to stand a certain distance away from the door after class so that I could have enough space to open it. I told them, "Don't touch my door." As expected, there were always some students who wanted to test the boundaries of the new rule by deliberately touching my door as they left the classroom. I then asked them to return to the classroom, go to the end of the line, and apologize to the door before leaving.

From then on, it seemed that everyone started to accept the rule. Years later, from the principal to the new students of grade seven, everyone knew this golden rule "Don't touch Mr. Fan's door!" Even at the open evening every year, I would pick two students in grade seven and ask them to announce this rule to visiting parents and their kids. Although they found it a bit weird, they still chose to obey the rule.

Because I rarely explained to students or their parents why they shouldn't touch my door, they started to try and guess the reason themselves. A lot of people think it must be related to Chinese culture or superstition. Once, I explained the story behind this rule to a curious parent. She understood that I had created it so that students would show respect to teachers and their teaching process.

As time passed, the rule became a part of our school's culture which also reflects the profound impact of Chinese teaching. The initial confusion and curiosity around my door turned into respect and recognition. This seemingly simple rule exemplifies mutual understanding, trust and respect between teachers and students. As a Chinese teacher, I teach them Chinese, and moreover, I teach them how to understand and embrace different cultures and rules.

About the author

Fan Xuequn started self-education after working as a foundry worker. In 1999, Fan earned a bachelor's degree in finance from Shanghai University of Finance and Economics. In 2000, he went to study in the UK and obtained an MBA from the University of Hertfordshire in 2001. In 2015, Fan completed his PGCE at the Institute of Education at UCL and became the first Chinese teacher at Melbourn Village College after graduation. Fan was honored with the Excellence Award by the UCL Confucius Institute. Now he is the head of the foreign languages department at the school and takes charge of promoting Chinese in the CAM Academy Trust.

Are You Alright?

Written by: Wen Diya
Translated by: Shuhan Cheng

My husband is British. After we got married, we lived in a terraced house in Brighton; a two-hundred-year-old building called Fisherman's Cottage where fishermen once lived. The house was small yet lovely, with a tiny front yard and a rose garden. Seated upstairs, we often saw tourists shamelessly snapping photos of it. Occasionally, however, they'd "take the piss" (pun intended) and pee on our doorstep! I understand that there is a dearth of public toilets along Brighton's seaside, and that the holly trees in our front garden provide the perfect cover, but I found it deeply uncomfortable to see people having a wee in our front garden.

The idea of confronting a trespassing tinkler was mortifying to me, but one day, while my husband was home, I made him do it.

"Are you alright?" he said to our unwelcome visitor, who was still shaking out his willy.

"Sorry, I really couldn't hold it!" replied the interloper.

Then, without another peep from my husband, the man zipped up and walked away.

Over the many years I've spent in Britain, I've learned that the British (and especially my very British husband) are not willing to face conflict head on. They much prefer to dance around it, thereby maintaining the decorum and propriety that they hold in such great esteem. I know that if I hadn't urged my husband to go outside and confront the man "watering" our garden, he never would have. He'd rather try and redesign the garden to prevent it from happening than tell someone off who was clearly in the wrong.

In many ways, my husband isn't any different from the affable protagonist played by Hugh Grant in the classic British film *Notting Hill*. When Grant's character encounters troublesome people in the bookshop where he works or when his friends and family embarrass him, he never protests. It's the British way. Some may say it's gentlemanly, but I find it confusing.

For example, when invited to an event, the British may respond subtly, saying "I'll think about it" or "I've got plans and I'm not sure if I can make it".

They often use ambiguous language, especially when discussing sensitive topics or controversial issues, preferring vague terms to avoid direct arguments. They might say, "That's an interesting view, but I see it a bit differently" or "I don't quite agree with you". They express their opinions indirectly, perhaps saying, "I'm not sure this is the right idea for us", or "Maybe we could consider other options". Then they lay out a multitude of options, so that their real choice or opinion can be artfully camouflaged among them.

Their sense of humour is also distinctively British. They often choose to defuse conflicts and tensions with self-deprecating humour.

In daily life, this can all be quite mind-boggling. Their lack of a direct answer doesn't mean they don't have one – it just requires a bit of sleuthing and familiarity with British society in order to decode.

As we know, the characteristics of a nation's people are shaped by various factors, such as history, culture, traditions and customs, etc. In the past, I have read several books by British authors about the characteristics of the British people. Based on my understanding, I would like to offer a brief analysis for further reflection from the following perspectives:

British culture values politeness and respect for others' feelings, always striving to avoid causing inconvenience or offence. Therefore, they prefer to solve problems through dialogue and compromise rather than confrontation.

Historically, the UK has been a country with a strict social hierarchy. To maintain social order and respect others' status, the British have tended to avoid conflicts and preserve social harmony. Even today, there are many "codes of behaviour" and unwritten "rules" between various "classes". Although these behavioural codes are gradually fading, especially in large cities with increasing foreign populations, "Britishness" remains widespread among the British people. In addition, Britain has a long-standing tradition of non-violence, which has influenced British behaviour. They are more inclined to resolve disputes through legal and rational approaches rather than through intense confrontation.

Therefore, British people rarely complain in public. It's not that they don't have complaints; they are just more likely to joke about their unhappiness with each other and then let it go. Many of my Chinese friends have observed that when you get stern with British people, they are often at a loss. Indeed, they don't particularly know how to deal with emotional responses (which are quite normal in many contexts in China), and their instinct is to avoid direct conflict. If only they would avoid our holly trees!

About the author

Wen Diya has been a columnist for various magazines for many years. During her time as a reporter and host of CCTV's news commentary programme *Oriental Horizon*, specifically for the "Oriental People" segment, she published two books: *Wen Diya Interviews* and *Wen Diya Diaries*. Later, she pursued her studies in the UK, where she obtained three master's degrees and collaborated with Phoenix Satellite Television to produce the series *European Tour*. Currently, she is a contributing correspondent for Hong Kong magazine *Ming Pao Monthly* in the UK. During the pandemic, she has been regularly posting articles on her WeChat public account "Miss Wen's Aerobic Garden" about physical and mental health, personal growth, and parenting, which have received widespread attention, especially from overseas Chinese. She enjoys painting, hiking and sea swimming, and is actively involved in social activities with various local charities and Chinese associations.

Theatre in London: A Must-See Experience

Written by: Ding Xuan
Translated by: Hanhan Xu

In the theatre, I smile, applaud, ponder and pay tribute.

My favourite pastime in London is indulging in theatrical performances at century-old venues, where I enjoy everything from dramas and musicals to stage plays and live rap shows.

During my time in the UK, I've found immense enjoyment in attending theatre performances and rarely miss shows featuring prominent actors or renowned theatre companies. While I typically base my choices on critics' reviews, there are times when a play's title alone draws me in, hoping for a soul-stirring surprise. The theatre arts section in newspapers is essential reading for me, and my inbox is always filled with newsletters about upcoming shows, thanks to my subscriptions to numerous theatre websites. My passion for theatre fuels all of this, as you can imagine.

British stage plays have a long-standing tradition of continuous development and innovation. They cover a vast array of topics, from Medieval Biblical drama from the Middle Ages and Shakespearean works to contemporary social issues, blending aesthetics with modern technology. Over time, the form, venues and social significance of British theatre have evolved alongside historical progress. While I am far from an expert in this field and consider myself just an audience member, I have a deep appreciation for the captivating experience offered by live performances, beautifully designed stages, and live music crafted specifically for these productions.

I still vividly remember a winter night in London, years ago, when I left the theatre after a show and stepped back into the world outside. Wrapped in my overcoat, I walked home through the gentle rain, shimmering under the glow of yellow streetlights, with the lively clacking of my boots on the cobblestone alleyways of the West End. The melodies of the performance still lingered in my mind. It was a moment of pure joy and contentment, so surreal that I couldn't help but wonder if life itself was as meticulously choreographed as a play.

As a child, I lived with my grandparents, both avid readers of Western literature. After spending my youth immersed in English novels, life eventually brought me here, to Britain – specifically to the theatres of London, adorned with red velvet and golden wood carvings. I found myself discovering new stories, meeting fresh characters, laughing, and being inspired by thought-provoking dialogue. Life, it seems, has a way of weaving stories we never could have anticipated.

In London, plays typically have long runs at a single theatre. Stage sets and cast members often remain at the same theatre for extended periods – months, years, or even decades. As a case in point, a theatre near my home is proudly celebrating the 70th anniversary of *The Mousetrap* – a crime thriller – this year. The same play is performed almost every day of the week, sometimes even twice a day. Theatre entrances are always brightly lit, bustling with people eager to watch. Inside, there are always shows playing. An interesting aspect of London is that to become a cab driver, one must memorise all the productions that theatres are hosting as part of a test. If you want to take a cab to visit the theatre, all you need to do is let the driver know the play you are going to watch. If you do not believe me, ask a cabbie and see for yourself.

In my experience attending numerous plays in London – ranging from dramas and operas to ballets, pantomimes and experimental theatre – I've never seen a sparse audience. Sitting in those antique theatre chairs, it's clear that theatre is a fundamental part of British life and culture. This vibrant theatre scene consistently draws in diverse audiences, fuelling the passion and talent of playwrights, set designers and actors alike. For any foreigner, it's an experience not to be missed.

Many renowned actors from around the world take great pride in having performed in plays and musicals in London. They view it as an invaluable opportunity to refine their craft and receive immediate feedback from a discerning audience. I've witnessed performances by distinguished actors who gave their absolute best on stage, earning the admiration and respect of every enthusiastic audience member who had come to appreciate their artistry.

Seeing a play in the UK isn't cheap. For popular or new productions, especially those featuring famous actors, ticket prices can range from tens to hundreds of pounds, depending on the seating. Even for long-running or niche performances, it's rare to find tickets in the single digits. While queuing for entry, I often think about how buying a ticket and attending a play is a significant expense for many. This makes the dedication of the cast all the more touching – they always strive to deliver captivating performances to ensure the audience feels they've gotten their money's worth.

I have a Welsh friend who works as a driver. Despite his muscular build and rugged job, he has a heart of gold. He chooses simpler, more affordable coffee and snacks to save money, yet he never misses a chance to take his wife to the theatre when she joins him for the weekend in London. He often tells me, with a beaming smile, about how much they enjoy these outings together. His joy is infectious and serves as a reminder of the simple pleasures in life.

Some people attend the theatre alone. Occasionally, I am one of them, finding joy in my own company. In my view, a night in the theatre is best spent with friends, family or a partner. But one can also find pleasure in watching performances alone if the experience is about appreciating the performances and getting immersed in the stories. There's no need to compromise on the choice of plays or to dissect each other's thoughts afterwards. It's simply about being present in the moment and enjoying the performance, free from distractions.

Between 2020 and 2021, the world ground to a halt, and theatres were among the first to close, delivering a devastating blow to the careers and livelihoods of countless performers in the industry. London's once-bustling streets became eerily quiet, yet now and then, the silence was broken by the haunting melodies of singers or the sight of impromptu performances by professional artists. Though they had turned to street performances out of necessity, their live art brought a much-needed touch of warmth and vibrancy to an otherwise frozen, lifeless world.

In 2022, COVID restrictions were lifted in London and performances gradually resumed. I picked a new play to celebrate my return as an audience member. The play was *Pride & Prejudice * (*sort of)*, a niche comedy with an all-female cast. I loved everything about it – the plot, the acting, and the creativity involved. When the audience gave a standing ovation at the end, I found myself smiling with tears of joy, not just because of the play, but the sight of the artists back on stage.

As I write this, winter has just begun in London. By four or five in the afternoon, it's already dark and cold, with chilling winds and rain driving people into the warmth of indoor spaces. I can't help but think that such grim weather must have played a role in shaping British literature and theatre. Reading by the fireplace is a solitary pleasure, while attending a play is a shared delight. Since joy is always greater when shared, why not head to the theatre and immerse yourself in the experience?

About the author

Ding Xuan shuttles between the East and West, residing outside of China. She is passionate about the arts and humanities.

"Black Tea, No Milk, Ta"

Written by: Tian Tian

Having a "cuppa" in the UK is quite an arduous task, and even after a decade here, the British way of tea drinking still feels exotic to me. Walking into a tiny café, I order a breakfast tea, and soon a waitress appears with a giant tray balanced on her slim arms. On the tray sits a hefty white ceramic cup, dominating the small saucer beneath it. A tiny milk jug perches inside the cup, accompanied by shiny accessories: a small teaspoon and, on occasion, a whimsical silver strainer or infuser.

You can hear this clattering medley of metal and ceramic before you see it: as the waitress's arms tremble, the teapot lid bumps against the rim, and the little spoon dances frantically on the saucer's edge. This noisy ensemble is so lively that you might mistake the teapot for a boiling kettle. The music continues as the tea is served: the clinking of cups and pots, the pouring of tea and milk, the scooping and dropping of sugar, and the stirring – all produce their own distinct notes. Finally, after what feels like an eternity, you get to take that triumphant sip.

In East Asia, there is a different Way of Tea: the Chinese bathe their burnished red tea pets in an endless flow of black tea, while the Japanese whisk away time with vibrant green matcha. But this noisy, homely ritual is undoubtedly the British Way of Tea.

When I first arrived in the UK, I distanced myself from the British way of drinking tea. Coming from China, the birthplace of tea, I assumed there was nothing I could learn from the British. Before my long journey west, my father – a devoted tea drinker who once sipped from his cherished Yixing earthenware teapot – squeezed a tiny porcelain teapot into my backpack. Shaped like a lovely lotus, its petals wrapped around the body, with the seed head serving as the lid. It was a charming design for solitary drinkers: if you flipped the lid upside down, it transformed into a small teacup, ready for use. I once envisioned myself sipping tea absentmindedly among books in some cosy London nook.

However, that romantic notion was quickly shattered by the hectic life of a PhD student. Tea soon transformed from a cultural beverage requiring patience and contemplation into a mere elixir to stave off sleepiness and idleness. Each morning, still half-asleep, I would reach for a teabag from the carton, toss it into a mug, and douse it with boiling water until it swelled and floated in the dark liquid. Just a few gulps were all it took to down that murky potion, and the entire process felt utterly wretched.

Despite the degradation in my tea consumption, I clung to one last shred of dignity: no milk in my tea. I firmly believe that tea should never mingle with milk, a stubborn idiosyncrasy that makes me one of the most conservative tea drinkers around. When bubble milk tea invaded young Chinese palates with its sweet "boba" ammunition I refused to bow to its sugary tyranny.

Although I admire Mongolian "suutei tsai", which combines black tea with milk, salt, fried millet and assorted cheeses, I don't make this nomadic legacy a regular part of my diet. For me, tea should be simple: just a pot of water and a handful of tea leaves – nothing more.

Yet, I'm not the only one fussy about tea; the English are just as particular. Milk comes in a wide array of options: oat, soy, regular, or none at all. Sugar also has its choices: white, brown, sweetener, or none. The amount of sugar can range from "two spoonfuls" to "half a spoonful", but the definition of "spoonful" is equally varied: it can be level or heaped. Ordering tea becomes akin to deciphering a pedantic insurance policy.

No wonder humorists Stuart and Jenny Payne refer to this British eccentricity as "Tea Policy". This specificity often ties into social identity: a worker's tea is typically strong, with milk and two spoonfuls of sugar. Breaking someone's tea policy can be a bit embarrassing. Perhaps this is why the owner of a fish and chips shop in Hastings always appears as alert as a meerkat when I order my tea, one hand gripping a notepad while the other flits about, scribbling down every detail.

My tea policy could be one of the simplest on this island: just TEA, and nothing else. Yet this straightforward stance led to many clashes with the British milk-tea policy and resulted in some amusing situations.

During my first year in London, I was a master's student living in a catered hall with the grand name of Ifor Evans. Every morning, I would stroll into the dining room, my habitual slumberous face in tow, and receive the generous English breakfast offerings from the catering staff. Bacon and sausage were delightful additions at first, but after a couple of months, they became too greasy for me. The only way to wash them down was with a mug of tea from the hot drinks machine, a reliable yet mediocre establishment.

I would pick up a faceless white mug from its blue plastic home, press the button, and watch as a steamy, inky elixir trickled down with a buzz – black tea without any personality, but it happened to be my cup of tea, quite literally.

As I washed down my greasy breakfast with that black potion, I had no idea a pair of eyes had been watching me for some time. They belonged to a sturdy janitor in a blue T-shirt, who stood guard at the entrance every day, holding his mop like St. George. One morning, he quietly approached, pulled out the chair across from me, and sat down, his onyx-like eyes fixed intently on me. Then he spoke cautiously, as if addressing a skittish fawn:

"I've been watching you for half a year, and I have to ask you one thing."

"Okay," I replied, thinking he might want to learn a few Chinese words.

His gaze dropped to my mug. "Why do you drink your tea without milk?"

It was an unexpected question. Caught off guard, I responded hastily, as if a tribe member were answering an anthropologist, "I've been drinking tea like this since childhood; it's just my habit."

Our amateur anthropologist seemed satisfied and nodded before quietly slipping away. That interaction made me realise that every habit is rooted in something deeply embedded in the collective consciousness of society, and tea drinking is no exception. My no-milk policy champions the bitterness of black tea: sip a mouthful, let it linger, allowing the bitterness to invade every corner of your palate until it's glazed with tannins, and only then can you swallow. Afterward, you exhale, and an astonishing aroma suddenly emerges at the back of your nose.

This way of drinking resonates with a particular virtue that Chinese culture has prized for centuries: "Eating Bitterness", a term for "sucking it up". Only by experiencing bitterness can one truly appreciate the rewarding sweetness that follows. Hence, while British nanny Mary Poppins sings, "A spoonful of sugar helps the medicine go down," her Chinese counterpart might say, "A spoonful of sugar after the medicine has gone down".

In pursuit of this virtue, I became a sort of flagellant, seeking out bitterness in life. My first few years in London were a bountiful quarry of miseries. Days were devoted to research and writing, while nights were spent reading and translating. I worked until my shoulders and neck protested violently with pain. Then, one November evening, I ventured out for some fresh air. Crippled by exhaustion, I dragged my weary body down Amwell Street beneath gloomy clouds that contrasted sharply with the golden autumn leaves. Suddenly, the clouds broke, and golden beams of the setting sun shot through. At that moment, I saw it: the slender Gothic tower of St. Mark, gilded by the dying sun, piercing the grey firmament. For me, this was the rewarding fragrance that followed the bitter taste.

The British, however, seem to avoid even the slightest bitterness in their tea, adding milk not only for flavour but to suppress that bitterness altogether. This tendency reflects their lifestyle: there's always something to counter life's bitterness – a tea break, even if it's in paper cups at the office with colleagues, a casual chat during lunch, mindless wandering among colourful boutiques, or chewing the fat over a pint with friends in a pub. I stood aloof from this lifestyle, just as I avoided milk in my tea. I often questioned how such a seemingly leisurely people could have built a great nation that once shook the world.

The British, in turn, didn't care for my tea policy; busy baristas would always hand me white tea. Later, in a moment of desperation, I shouted

"Black tea" over the bustling noise in the café, but only the syllables "La" and "Tea" managed to penetrate the filter of loud music and chatter.

There's always a dash of milk in the tea of my life here. In my third year of study in London, I met my future wife, and we've been inseparable ever since, even in cafés. Each morning, we would order a cup of black tea, no milk, and share it together. She encouraged me not to work through the nights and weekends, reminding me to enjoy life. My Scottish supervisor, though often critical, taught me how to savour a scone and eventually introduced me to her newborn son. Gradually, the milk of love and friendship seeped into my tea.

One day, my wife said, "Darling, how about a white tea?" Surprisingly, I didn't resist. The musical clinking of spoons and cups has become a familiar soundtrack at our table. Why should I cling to my tea?

About the author

Tian Tian is an archaeologist, historian and an avid reader.

The Taste of Sandwiches

Written by: Zhe'an
Translated by: Dan Wu

In the first year or two after I arrived in the UK, I thought sandwiches were the most unpalatable food I could ever encounter. The three syllables of this word made me think of another three syllables instead: not tasty. It also became a puzzle to me. How can two slices of dry bread filled with some half-cooked, tasteless meat, cheese and lettuce make it to rows and rows of space on supermarket shelves, each costing several pounds? These were the days when one pound converted to twelve Chinese yuan, where I could have afforded a decent hot meal with soup and stir-fried dishes in China at the same price.

Long before I relocated to the UK, I already learnt about the origin of sandwiches. The rumour goes that during the 18th century, the 4th Earl of Sandwich was so addicted to gambling that he had no time to leave the table for a meal, so he always grabbed a bite with some bread and meat. Although we are not sure of the reliability of the story, it fits the stereotype of British cuisine: the tastiness of food is not very important.

Leaving tastiness to one side, still, sandwiches do not seem to fulfill even the least I would have expected from food – to make people feel full. Even now, I am still surprised when I see a strong and powerfully-built Brit carefully biting into a sandwich. Some of my British friends gave me a consistent reason as to why they don't eat much: eating half keeps them awake in the afternoon. Indeed, unlike in some Chinese workplaces, Brits don't sleep at noon. Most people go off work at a fixed time, and many would rather catch up on work during their lunch break with a sandwich than staying in the office for overtime after five p.m.

What I needed the most during my school days was calories. However, the school canteen always provided the same food: cold salads or jacket potatoes with baked beans. And so, I began to explore the world of sandwiches.

As a student without deep pockets, I was looking for good value for money, which meant more calories for the same price. Following this rule, a sandwich with bacon, lettuce and tomato was definitely my top go-to choice. There's something endearingly British about its full name, Classic BLT – as if sandwiches, like the literary world, have to be spelt out between classic masterpieces and ordinary creations. Another two choices were Cheese and Onion and Prawn Mayo. But Cheese and Ham or Egg and Watercress both often left me half-full and failed to feed me. As for Tuna and Sweetcorn, despite the cheerful name in its Chinese translation, it had a fishy flavour that I'd run away from.

My attitude towards sandwiches came about because of a vegetarian sandwich called Ploughman. At first, this sandwich didn't catch my eye. The reason, I'm ashamed to say, was simply because I didn't recognise the word "ploughman". While other sandwiches have self-explanatory names, this had a special one. As I went on living in the UK for a number of years, I started getting used to the lifestyle here, and managed to squeeze out available energy to learn more words and explore things around me, and subsequently was able to scratch some details from beneath the surface. So then, one day, I finally discovered this sandwich.

The description revealed that it contained cheddar cheese, pickle, tomato and lettuce with mustard and chutney. I didn't have high expectations. However, after one bite into the sandwich, the pungency of the mustard, the sourness and saltiness of the pickle, and the soft, sweet flavour of the cheddar cheese awakened my taste buds. I was pleasantly surprised – sandwiches could be tasty after all!

Sandwiches hold such importance for British people that they are often used as a metaphor in daily life. After my studies, and a few years later, I was working in London. I had to both give and receive feedback from colleagues at all levels for my annual appraisal. My predecessor, who mentored me, suggested that good feedback should look like a "sandwich" in order to be acknowledged: it should start and end with positive recognition, encouragement, or constructive comments, with any issues to be raised in the middle. I once heard a British colleague say, "Just tell me the stuff in the middle!" Most of the time, however, this can be a tried and tested format of communication. If a person is too direct in the workplace, people might laugh and think it's too American, or "like a bull in a china shop."

This kind of thinking may be easy for the Brits, but I had to learn it. For a while, my role involved business development for an accountancy firm. I worked like an octopus, responding to emails, WeChat messages and phone calls externally, while coordinating, translating and delegating internally, all of which was on top of delivering my own allocated work. In the past, I converted every pound into effective calories, and here I was, trying to turn every minute into effective work! One British colleague who worked with me was a senior manager a few years older than me. He was fluent in Chinese, and his Chinese surname was based on his Chinese wife's surname. I have to say that he was indeed progressive. I treated him almost as a compatriot, as if a cultural barrier did not exist.

After becoming friendly with him, I would discuss work with him directly when I met him occasionally. However, I realised that no matter how rushed I was, he would always engage me in small talk and ask about my weekend plans before saying goodbye.

I thought it was some kind of daily routine and a simple "I'm fine" or a short polite reply would be enough. If you really go on and on about your plans for the weekend, it may be frustrating for the other person. Once, I couldn't help asking him why he couldn't just go straight to the work topic, given that we were close friends and that we had a lot of work to do.

I couldn't forget the moment when he turned seriously to me and said, word for word: "These greetings are very important."

These words took root in my mind at a steady pace, much like the slow-changing scenery of a street in the UK. Many years later, I finally came to understand this way of communication through the simple, everyday object that is the sandwich. The casual small talk at the beginning and end, seemingly mundane, brings a calm, steady and unhurried rhythm to conversations. Gradually, I began to understand why everything in the UK, from food and product packaging to fashion, tends to favour simplicity. It is precisely this simplicity that allowed the UK, when faced with the challenge of World War II, to tell its people, "Keep calm and carry on."

In recent years, I have unexpectedly discovered something new happening to me. Perhaps because I have long been accustomed to flavours that are not as strong, I now find sandwiches delicious. I have come to appreciate the original taste of the ingredients, such as the texture of fresh wholewheat bread, the clean and crisp lettuce and tomato slices, and beef seasoned simply with salt and pepper. I have also found sandwiches with delightful names besides the classic Ploughman's, such as "Coronation Chicken", which was created for Queen Elizabeth II's coronation in 1953 and later became a popular sandwich filling. Sandwiches have evolved with the time; varieties with avocado, which were unheard of twenty years ago, are now ubiquitous.

In June 2023, while on a business trip back to China, I enjoyed lavish meals for two weeks straight. As I was about to return to the UK, I suddenly craved the simplest, most refreshing sandwich to cleanse my palate. In the downtown area of early summer Shanghai, I searched under the clear blue sky but only found a kind of sandwich with thick mayonnaise. It won't hurt, I thought. Think of the 4th Earl of Sandwich three hundred years ago – just having something to eat is good enough. Besides, it would still be tastier than the tuna and sweetcorn option for me.

About the author

Zhe'an is a Chartered Tax Advisor and partner at a top accounting firm in the UK. She is the author of the novel *Floating Lights, Moving Water*, which depicts the lives of contemporary Chinese people in the UK.

My British In-Laws

Written by: He Yue
Translated by: Kaidi Lyu

When I first visited my British in-laws, their lifestyle was a real eye-opener. It was 2008, and at the time, I had no idea that so many British people preferred living in the countryside. I associated the countryside with poverty and backwardness. My in-laws lived in the countryside, surrounded by fields, cattle, sheep, and a national protected forest, with a golf course right next door. To me, modernity meant skyscrapers, so I couldn't comprehend how cattle and sheep could coexist with a golf course. I also couldn't understand why my in-laws would choose to live in the countryside and yet have such modern appliances. When my mother visited a few years later, she asked a typical Chinese question, "Aren't you worried about safety in such a remote place?" My father-in-law, a businessman, smiled and replied, "We Brits are used to paying high taxes and sharing with the poor. That's how we keep society stable." At that time, my understanding of British capitalism was very basic. My thinking was still stuck on the idea that "it doesn't matter if a cat is black or white, as long as it catches mice." I found my father-in-law to be incredibly generous and progressive. Back then, I aspired to be a well-heeled, uniformed, high-ranking white-collar worker, believing Britain to be the "most class-conscious society" as rumoured in China. I didn't realise how high labour costs in the UK were and assumed that all middle-class families had maids. My in-laws' house was huge, but apart from a gardener, they did everything themselves – cooking, laundry and housework. My father-in-law had a massive garage full of various power tools, which he called his toy room. I found it incredible – he wore a suit to work, but at home, he'd change into work clothes and tinker in the garage, often getting dirty. I had never even seen a lawnmower before, and he had ten of them, ranging from mini to car-sized, electric to diesel. His favorite pastime was "mowing the lawn up and down the hills", which I couldn't imagine being fun. Many years later, I learned that walking or taking the dog out to "get some fresh air" is the British equivalent of the Chinese "taking a walk" – just a normal part of daily life. Chinese people might find this puzzling and wonder why British people don't just open the window? Why complicate things? The answer, which might be hard for Chinese people to accept, is that Britain is cold, especially in winter, and homes need to retain as much heat as they can, so windows are rarely opened. When my mother visited Britain every year, she felt suffocated if she couldn't open the window daily. My husband couldn't understand, "How could you feel suffocated without opening the window?"

Watching my mother-in-law manage the household, I felt like she could run a small hotel. The things I had to call a property maintenance person for back in China, she handled effortlessly. This made me feel especially inadequate as a woman – I felt like all I could do was study. She would often tease me as being "useless". Born in the 1950s, my mother-in-law's generation experienced the happiest, most liberated and egalitarian era for everyday British citizens: the 1960s with The Beatles and miniskirts. Her outdated clothes looked both fashionable and beautiful to me. Her exquisite bone china tableware and tea sets, once popular, are now either displayed or stored away. She and her husband drank tea and coffee from large mugs, which I initially thought was unrefined. Later, I understood that the bone china items, vintage clothes and Rococo-style furniture popular in China are no longer in vogue in Britain. Today's Britain is a post-class society where "convenience" has replaced old-fashioned "refinement". My in-laws enjoyed cooking various international dishes and appreciated each other's efforts. Watching them cook Chinese food, I saw it wasn't authentic but somewhat close. They had no concept of the precise heat control essential in Chinese cuisine. The UK's strict safety standards make the British sensitive to fire hazards. Stir-frying onions and garlic on extremely high heat, as is regularly done in Chinese cooking, shouldn't be done in front of the British – it might scare them. I heard that when the famous Chinese-American TV chef Ken Hom cooked Chinese food for the BBC in 1984, they had the fire brigade on standby.

Back then, I thought that the aristocracy was still a significant social force and that dressing formally was necessary to gain respect. For my parents' first visit to my in-laws' house, I specifically asked them to dress nicely to avoid embarrassment. Looking back now, none of that was necessary. My father-in-law is a very relaxed person and loves to joke – he even discusses things like death as casually as the weather. Now that I can understand his jokes and laugh out loud, I realise how tense I was when I first got to England. When meeting and saying goodbye to my in-laws, I had to kiss them, and initially, I was very stiff. My mother-in-law's kisses and hugs were warm and loving, and now I've learned to express about half of that affection. Mentally, I've also become very relaxed. It's hard to explain, but I feel like my mind and body have been liberated. Now, my mother-in-law no longer calls me useless. She once said she was surprised I dared to come to the UK to study alone. She was probably also surprised that I eventually adapted to so many local customs. It only took me about twenty years! But one thing is clear – the real Britain and the Britain portrayed in Chinese textbooks are two completely different places. I'm glad I get to live in the former.

About the author

He Yue is a columnist for the *Financial Times* Chinese website, political commentator for *Lianhe Zaobao* and *South China Morning Post*, member of the UK Labour Party and member of the UK National Union of Journalists.

Pants, Underpants and Other Humorous Differences Between British and American English

Written by: Du Yubin
Translated by: Guo Hongfei

In the autumn of 2019, I moved to the UK after working in Washington for a long time. I always imagined that since the US and the UK shared a language, I was unlikely to experience culture shock. I was wrong! During my time in London I encountered not only cultural shock, but also embarrassing cultural jokes. As a Chinese person who lived in both the UK and the US, I experienced the cultural difference between the East and the West, and also between the US and the UK. Once shared, such experience may inspire insights and thoughts in others. Even as a joke it can be worth a try.

On my first day at the office, I chatted with my British colleagues and we engaged in some small talk about where we lived. Two middle-aged male colleagues, far away from their beloved girlfriends, said that they shared the same flat in order to save money. After hearing this I replied, "You two are colleagues and roommates!"

Both of them blushed with awkwardness and explained, "Just to make things clear, we are flatmates, not roommates. We live in separate rooms." Only then did it occur to me that "roommate" was from American-English, and referred to people sharing the same house but not necessarily the same room. In British English, the word "roommate" was interpreted more literally.

I burst into laughter and explained that I hadn't realized that the same word had two different meanings. Little did I know, there were many English words that I needed to "re-learn" in England. Whereas the Americans call a knitted top a sweater, Brits call it a jumper. Likewise,

Americans say eggplant and Brits use the French aubergine, to refer to the same vegetable. Football versus soccer, trash can versus bin. The examples are endless. And so are the ambiguities.

One day after work, I went to pick up my bike with a colleague. I mentioned that it was raining so heavily that my pants got wet. He started to laugh uncontrollably and said, "Do you mean your trousers?" I said of course, what else? He continued to explain that pants in Britain meant underwear. Though the British would understand either word, their first reaction to hearing "pants" would be to think "underwear". He then joked, "What made your underwear wet?" Fortunately he was a friend who knew me well, or a misunderstanding like this would have been very embarrassing.

Unfortunately, what scares you the most often comes after you. I did embarrass myself once in public as a result of using the wrong word. By public, I mean Number 9 Downing Street, where the Press Briefing Room is located, right next to Number 10, the official residence of the British Prime Minister. On that day I went to the press conference. I arrived early and still had some time to go to the loo.

I asked the staff there, "Excuse me, where is the restroom please?" A new office lady politely asked me to wait so that she could ask for permission. After two minutes, she came back and said, "I will lead the way since there is still time before the press conference." I was surprised that I needed to be escorted to the loo, but I followed the lady across various hallways, climbed many stairs and finally saw the sign for the loo. Right as I was about to dash in, the lady stopped me and said, "Not here sir. Please follow me." She then guided me to the REST ROOM.

She opened the door for me. I looked in and saw a security guard resting there who had just finished his lunch. Annoyance and laughter seized me at the same time. I just wanted to use the toilet, but apparently she hadn't understood me. While in American English the restroom refers to the toilet, in British English, it can be easily interpreted as a room for rest.

In recent years, gender and sexuality have prompted many debates in western societies. I feel that the UK is paying particular attention to these debates by adjusting public expressions that may arouse concern.

For example, the word spokesman and spokeswoman have now become spokesperson. In the UK, sexuality is never a hindrance to love. Civil partnership is evidence of this. I once believed that such categorisation was specifically set for same-sex couples.

A colleague of mine often mentioned his partner, so I always thought he was gay. Then one day we had a chat and he said, "I am going to get married!" I congratulated him, "That's amazing! Congratulations to you and your boyfriend. You guys must have been through a lot." Hearing that, his jaw dropped and he replied, "I'm marrying a woman!" He then explained to me that the neutral word partner was used to avoid discrimination with regards to sexuality.

These days, many people use the word partner to refer to their other half, instead of saying boyfriend, girlfriend, husband or wife. So the next time you hear someone saying partner, don't be surprised or make any assumptions like I did.

In the UK, people use "what a shame" or "shame" a lot, which sounds like disgrace, a negative expression. It is said that this phrase often reminds many Chinese of a mean middle-aged woman who often appears in western movies and publicly shames a poor man who has a different religion or tradition. However, in reality, this phrase is only used to describe a pity, so a more precise translation into Chinese would be "what a pity". This one is also used by Americans so it's worth remembering – you can avoid confusion in two countries!

Though cultural differences are inevitable, the longer I live abroad, the more I realise how much we have in common with people on the other side of the world. Although we may have different names for things, there is so much we can learn from one another, even if there are a few language hiccups along the way.

About the author

Du Yubin is a reporter for CGTN (China Global Television Network) stationed in the UK, part of China Media Group. His Channels on WeChat: *Xiaodu's Big World* – how China views the world and how the world views China.

Britain is Old Fashioned, isn't It?

Written by: Gu Hongyan
Translated by: Wang Luyu

In the spring of 2017, I was about to travel from Nanjing to London. An old colleague wished me a smooth journey and asked, "Is air pollution still bad in London?" Being a literature enthusiast, he had read many of Dickens' books. Perhaps *Oliver Twist* left an indelible impression on his mind. For a place you have never visited, preconceived notions about the place are often based on literary works, movies, TV shows, news, the internet and hearsay.

What is life in the UK really like? I set off on the journey to immerse myself in British culture. It strikes me that unlike the Chinese, who are in a golden age of innovation, the British, in many ways, are still comfortably nestled into their traditional lifestyle, their old school and their old fashion.

Clothing, food, housing and transportation are vital to daily life. Let's start with clothing. Many of my Chinese colleagues would have brought back Burberry trench coats from the UK, as if the trench coats could give them a British flair. However, in Nanjing, people rarely have the chance to wear a trench coat. Although summer temperatures can easily exceed 35°C, in winter, you can feel the chill in your bones. As seasons of transition, the spring and autumn only last a few weeks. Especially during the rainy season, more than protection from the elements, a Burberry trench coat is more likely to cause heat rash, especially if worn in the humid alleyways of Jiangnan during rainy season.

I have lived in Somerset for more than six months this year. In late October, I visited the Hauser & Wirth gallery in Bruton, with my landlord Mark. The garden was surrounded by prickly shrubs covered in purple-grey berries. At first glance I thought they were blueberries, but Mark explained that they were sloes. "We can make sloe gin and enjoy a drink this Christmas," he said excitedly.

Sloe gin was mentioned in many novels I had read. I was keen to try it in person! Mark tried to pick the sloes off the prickly branches. There was a dense clump of berries high up that pricked his fingers when he grabbed them. I heard a ripping sound and saw that the left sleeve of his 25-year-old Barbour waxed jacket had been torn. Undeterred, he poured our spoils into his big jacket pockets and my straw hat. We ended up with 1.3 kg! Enough to fill a good-sized bottle.

The British believe in books. They follow recipes as if conducting a science experiment. Whereas Chinese recipes often call for a pinch of salt or a tablespoon of rice wine, British recipes include exact quantities of each ingredient. Thus, the British need to use kitchen scales and measuring cups for cooking. They also tend to follow instructions meticulously.

I suggested that Mark should repair his jacket. "I would rather not," he said. I then asked if he intended to buy a new one because the jacket was old. "Why? Its design is quite rare now. The two pockets are so practical! Perhaps I need to re-wax it", he replied. Barbour offers a service that allows their customers to return Barbour jackets at any time to be re-waxed, repaired or altered. Even the Queen used to walk her corgis wearing a headscarf and a Barbour jacket, just like any other Brit. Especially in the countryside, a Barbour jacket and a pair of Wellington boots are the ultimate in style.

When I first saw a pair of green Wellington boots at the writer Xinran's house, the boots had already trudged through plenty of mud in the English countryside. They became pots for green plants in her London home. The Wellington boots belonged to her husband, Toby Eady. Although Toby had been gone for years, his boots and lucky bamboo were still with his family.

I often hear people complain that British cuisine is too bland. They eat nothing but fish and chips! A wide range of British tableware may make up for this.

I once held an empty plate in the kitchen, and said to Mark, "You know, the willow tree plate reminds me of my hometown." "What? In China, there are widows in trees?" He asked, surprised. I immediately realised that he heard "widow" instead of "willow", due to my poor English. When he realised what had happened, he began laughing hysterically.

This joke was repeated to the merriment of others at the local pub. "Just for the willow tree, I went all the way to Stoke-on-Trent," I said.

Stoke-on-Trent is the home of Spode, a classic British ceramic brand that has been producing willow patterned tableware since the 1790s. I quipped that it was the UK's answer to Jingdezhen: China's ceramics hub. "Yes, of course, china from China," said Matthew, a local gardener and pub regular.

The intricate Chinoiserie willow pattern became popular in Britain in the late 18th century. At the time, British ceramic artists were inspired by luxury hand-painted blue-and-white porcelain imported from China. But rather than hand-painting their ceramics, the British printed their version of the pattern onto special paper, and then transferred the design from the paper to the ceramics. The same willow pattern they applied to the production of tableware has been in use for over 230 years.

Although there have been changes to some details over the years, the British willow pattern features a pair of birds, a bridge and a pavilion surrounded by trees. It may remind some Chinese people of Chinese poetry, but this was unlikely deliberate. More than poetry, the British are more focused on shapes and design. In the spring of 2020 I took a British willow plate to Suzhou because I wanted to show it what an auntentic Chinese classsical garden would look like.

In addition to tableware, the British love their countryside. Most people dream of owning a manor house, castle or even a simple country cottage. After a walk with your dog, you will see lintel and window panes surrounded by roses from afar on your way home. You open a wooden gate in your garden, and step into your house. In the house, a fireplace is burning bright, and a tea kettle whistles. You may want to enjoy a good cup of tea in the afternoon.

There is a Peony Cottage owned by an artist Nigel in Butleigh. The blue limestone walls are so thick that wi-fi doesn't get through the walls very well. Thus, routers need to be placed in accessible locations. The main house has a thatched roof. Peony Cottage is one of the oldest properties in the village of Butleigh, and a Grade II listed building. It was once the home of the Oscar-winning playwright Robert Bolt, who wrote *Lawrence of Arabia*, *Doctor Zhivago* and *A Man for All Seasons*. I once told Nigel that I had visited the Ashmolean Museum to see an Arab robe worn by T.E. Lawrence. He raised his eyebrows, smiled and said, "Well, you have already explored a lot in England."

Walking through the village, you can see various styles of cottages. Books are all freely available on outdoor wooden shelves, and clusters of lavender along garden walls often catch your feet. A giant ginkgo tree is in the east of the village. Gold leaves fall from the tree in late autumn, just like they do in China.

The village of Butleigh is lucky enough to have a wonderful trail around it. In the 1970s, a local historian called Ms. Ansell researched the big and small houses in the village. Nearly 30 of them were over 100 years old. The oldest extant building was a farmhouse by a bridge, which was built in the 16th century. Villagers created house plaques with interesting historical texts and property photos. For example, No. 17 High Street was a two-unit house built in the late 16th century. Charles Saddler rented the property – £5.5s in 1863 from Squire Neville-Grenville. By 1947, the rent had increased to £16.4s. Although the house signs were not placed in prominent positions, it was easy for pedestrians to find these house signs in gardens or on walls. Thus, it wasn't littered with ostentatious house plaques when you shot village photography. And your photos of the picturesque village aren't dominated with intrusive signs and flags. Later, the 500-year-old walking route in the village was named Ann Heeley Heritage Trail.

The more you see, the more you know.

About the author

Gu Hongyan is a volunteer at the Mothers' Bridge of Love and a traveller and learner.

In 2021, she obtained a master's degree in Cultural Heritage and Museum Studies at the University of East Anglia.

My Ten Years in the UK

Written by: Zhai Maona
Translated by: Rachel Cai

At the beginning of 2013, I embarked on my journey to the UK with my 7-month-old daughter. Her innocent smile and the heavy snowfall that year still live vividly in my memories of that time. Ten years have passed in a flash; it is now the last month of 2023. How many decades does one have in life? There are a few moments from these past ten years that I cherish the most...

After landing in the UK, our first meal was served at my husband's colleague's house. He and his wife were a lovely couple. Mr. Duan, affectionately known as "Brother Duan", was a Tsinghua alum, and his wife, "Sister Jia", was a Peking University alum, and a gentle and virtuous woman. She explained that lotus root, cabbage and tofu were considered "luxuries" in the UK. I was touched as I saw the table laden with these "luxuries". Being warmly welcomed in a foreign land was already a blessing, let alone being treated to an extravagant meal.

As I spent more time in the UK, I came to realise just how rare and precious lotus root, cabbage, and tofu truly are. I discovered that Haagen-Dazs and cabbage often cost the same, with almost every supermarket brimming with Haagen-Dazs, while finding a store that stocked cabbage can be quite the challenge. Whenever I reflect on that first meal, I feel an overwhelming sense of gratitude for Brother Duan and Sister Jia. We've embraced this spirit of hospitality ourselves, and with a constant influx of visiting scholars, welcoming and bidding farewell to guests has become a cherished part of our life here.

In the UK, I quickly grasped the meaning of the term "country on wheels". Here, it's quite rare to see someone carrying a child in their arms while out and about; instead, children are comfortably settled in strollers of all varieties, including single, double and even triple models. I once encountered a baby less than two weeks old playing at a children's centre. In China, a mother would never take her baby out during the postpartum one-month confinement period. That would be nothing short of a dream! Yet here, that dream becomes reality, as British women do not observe such confinement.

What truly struck me was how adults at many children's activity centres communicated with children at eye level. When the children sat, the adults sat; when the children kneeled or lay down, the adults followed suit. I couldn't help but wonder how this approach differs from what I might have seen in China, though I regret not having had children before to compare. I was pleasantly surprised, yet I didn't want to make a fuss. This profound respect for children's nature and their wishes, along with a strong emphasis on appreciation, encouragement and tolerance, was truly heartwarming. As a mother, I found it reassuring to see that the pressures of excessive early education or fierce competition, which I had often heard about, didn't appear to be prevalent here.

I have also witnessed the remarkable kindness of the British people. The first time I took my daughter to the city centre, I was unprepared for the complexity of the Underground lines and the numerous transfers. It was frustrating to discover that many transfers didn't have elevators. I regretted not doing enough research to understand the British Underground system better. As I stood staring at the stairs in despair, grumbling to myself, a gentleman in a long coat approached and asked, "I guess you need some help?" Before I could even respond, he had already lifted my daughter's stroller, carried it up the stairs, and escorted us to the entrance of the station.

Such kindness became a common occurrence, and I gradually grew accustomed to it. On one occasion, I was dragging a large, though not heavy, suitcase that I could have managed myself. However, as I paused for a moment to organise my clothes, someone swiftly picked up my suitcase and took it downstairs for me. I might have thought it was stolen if I hadn't grown used to such gestures of goodwill. There was even one time when

I genuinely thought my suitcase was being "stolen", only to discover that someone had carried it down for me, nodded at me, and disappeared before I could react – likely in a hurry.

Thanks to these heartwarming experiences, I've come to appreciate the worn charm of the British Underground system. After all, it's over a hundred years old, steeped in history and stories that span more than a century.

Over the past ten years, I've grown accustomed to not working overtime on weekends and embracing simple, relaxed relationships with my colleagues. Our gatherings have always been light-hearted and enjoyable. I want to give special mention to the somewhat old-fashioned tradition of Boxing Day. While employers may not typically give gifts to employees, our institute's big boss often invited us to his house parties, for which I am truly grateful – especially to his wife, whom I see as a virtuous woman.

I have also become accustomed to the sight of lush green water plants and snowy white swans. Among the Queen's private property, the swans are the birds I see most frequently, though I haven't looked into whether they now belong to the King after the Queen's passing. The British have a deep love for gardening, and their front and back yards are filled with a delightful array of flowers and plants. When my mother-in-law visited, she remarked that if we grew our own vegetables, we wouldn't need to rely on the supermarket. At the far end of our forty-metre-long yard, my diligent mother-in-law established a vegetable garden and embarked on her gardening endeavours. She often hums while tending to the plants, genuinely relishing the process. As a result, we've been able to enjoy completely natural, organic vegetables throughout the summer and early autumn, which not only fulfilled our needs but were also frequently shared with our neighbours.

Outdoors, you can often see people running everywhere – on the streets, in the forests, by the sea. Some even pick up litter as they run, holding empty bottles in their hands. I often wondered why they don't just carry a trash bag so they can carry even more.

Nowadays, the UK has become our partial homeland, with a significant decade of our lives spent here. I've grown accustomed to and come to cherish the slow pace of life, the inclusiveness, the gentility and the depth of this country. However, I'm still not a fan of the winters – when it rains, it feels as though the sky is leaking.

A few days ago, I went to replace a door handle. An elderly gentleman pulled out a thick book, carefully flipping through its pages before informing me that the handle style had been discontinued and that the same size was no longer available. If I insisted on changing the handle, I would need to replace the entire door. I explained that I didn't like the outdated style and wanted to change it. He shrugged, pushed up his glasses, looked at me intently and smiled, saying very solemnly, "Child, if you cannot change her, try to like her."

His words enlightened me. Change and growth can happen in an instant, and it was at that moment that I began to appreciate winter in England. Perhaps it was the way he began with "Child" that evoked the warmth of my parents and my homeland. I hope that you, dear reader, can also find your way to that warmth.

About the author

Zhai Maona was born in Shandong and graduated from Xiamen University. She moved to the UK in 2013 with her husband on a work visa to engage in research and education. In 2020, she transitioned to the health sector due to personal health issues. She is now a Senior Health Manager, Vice President of the Sino-German Nutrition and Health Association, and German PM Company UK branch president.

A Green Thumb

Written by: Liu Qian
Translated by: Christina Zhao

I always longed for an idyllic life in the countryside.

When I was a kid, my parents would always take me to my grandma's house for the weekend. Her home was nestled on the outskirts of Chengdu, in southwest China, where farmlands stretched out along the road in front of her house. One of my favourite activities was exploring the fields with Grandpa. He would hold my hand and point out which fields were planted with cotton and which with corn. I loved every moment of it and never grew tired of walking along the narrow, muddy countryside roads.

This is where my first impression of the countryside was formed – a cherished part of my childhood.

Three years ago, when I settled in the UK and finally had a garden of my own, it dawned on me that I could begin my own gentle, slow-paced, idyllic activity of farming. From the first spring in my new home, I've been deeply immersed in this pastime. Gardening, I've discovered, is almost an obsession among scholars in the UK. I recall, 13 years ago while pursuing my PhD, hearing Oxford professors say things like, "Dr. X not only has more publications but is also a better gardener than I", as a way of expressing admiration. It seemed that being a skilled gardener, even more than being a distinguished scholar, was an enviable accomplishment.

At that time I was sharing a house with two good friends of mine, and one of them was a doctoral supervisor who would bring us enormous courgettes that he grew himself every summer. Of course, we thanked the supervisor and his wife with the utmost respect in our traditional Chinese way – by preparing a homemade Sichuan hotpot. I must say, they were quite brave to try such bold flavours, and those shared moments were truly enjoyable for all of us.

I couldn't wait to start my own gardening. I bought some apple trees, pear trees, grape vines and strawberry plants online and planted them along the edges of the garden. My husband helped me loosen the soil to the south of the garden and then placed two wood blocks as borders. And voilà, garden done.

Since it was my first time planting vegetables, I didn't know much. I scattered the pea seeds in the field without even covering them with soil. Surprisingly, the peas grew anyway. I can still taste the sweetness of those peas when I think back to that spring. It wasn't only peas that were easy to grow. In the golden British summer, we could harvest one courgette every two days. We grew tomatoes and beans as well. From June to August, when the days can be as long as 17 hours, I was practically living in the garden. To me, picking vegetables was a joy. It was also my kids' favourite activity that summer.

I always joke that the point of planting vegetables is to grow things quickly. You reap what you sow, simple as that.

I have to say the reason planting brings me so much joy is that the two main pillars of my life require patience. For example, it takes almost 2 to 3 years to publish a paper or a book. It takes even longer to be a good parent.

However, planting is a whole different story. If you put a bag of peas into a plastic box with holes and put the box into a bigger one with a piece of wet kitchen towel on top, the peas will get bigger by the next morning. By the next morning, they'll have roots with hair. Within a week's time, you'll see 5cm tall, fresh green pea shoots. And you can add them to your noodles or your hotpot within two weeks. I began to understand why scholars in the UK love gardening. We like it, but we also need it. We need the enjoyment from planting, harvesting and the sweetness from the greens so that the long days of being an oftentimes "benched" scholar can feel more invigorating.

Last spring, I wanted to expand my "planting business" and even rented a piece of land near my home. I successfully persuaded friends to join us so we could co-plant this land. As it turned out, we had a lovely, busy but fulfilling time co-planting and harvesting.

My obsession with planting also had me joining a London-based planting group chat. The irony is I don't even live in London. Yes, that's how obsessed I was with planting. There is somebody we call "head of the village" in the group chat who knows everything about planting and would always answer questions thoroughly and thoughtfully. I discovered that he was also an Oxford graduate and that he had a lab in his garage where he experimented with lighting to increase yield.

Seeing people from impressive academic backgrounds share the same interest in planting and building connections brought me joy too. There was a girl I knew from the group who once gifted me a bunch of seedlings. In return, I gave her some seeds and a fig leaf gourd seedling. Six months later, I found my fig leaf gourd had become worm food, whereas hers was a success! She sent her husband to bring me half of it as she wanted to share the fruit of her success with me. Of course, we each cooked a half of it on the same evening to celebrate.

However, planting was not all I was passionate about. One day, I heard some hurried, faint noises coming from the grass on my way home after dropping the kids off at school. Upon closer inspection, I found a tiny black bird hopping around, looking very alone and lost. Not seeing any sign of a nest or a mother bird, I decided to bring it home. I fashioned a makeshift nest for the baby bird using a tissue box lined with soft tissues.

Unsurprisingly, my daughter was thrilled. She would carry the box around all day, chatting to the baby bird. Raising it wasn't easy at first; the bird refused to eat. After researching online, I learned that caring for a baby bird is quite similar to raising a baby – it requires patience. You can't force it to eat but must wait calmly. Eventually, the bird began to eat, just as children eventually adapt.

On that same day, we thought it'd be a good idea to take the box out in the garden and let the bird immerse itself in the natural surroundings. When we came back after leaving the house for just a few hours, all that was left for us was an empty box with some fur. The bird was nowhere to be found.

After this experience, I nearly embarked on another venture – raising hens. I bought a hen hut and called a farm about investing in some hens, but then realized that I'd never commit enough to chickens to avoid a disaster like the one with the small black bird. So I turned to tadpoles instead. I kept them in the bathtub until they grew up. We set them free in the pond at the university. Just as we let them go, a duck swam over. My younger daughter was worried the duck would eat her tadpoles. Every time we passed by that pond, my daughters would ask if the tadpoles were still there or if they had been eaten by the duck. We reassured them that the tadpoles swim very fast and were likely fine.

My apple and prune trees give plenty of fruit every autumn, which is a marvellous feeling. I have two prune plum trees, and one of them was gifted to me by my housemate's supervisor's wife when we first settled here. My supervisor passed away 7 years ago, but the tree has grown higher than the fence and makes me feel connected to him.

Now, that I'm a more seasoned gardener, I've learned to make peace with two things: the bugs eating my plants and being "benched". I have learned to be at peace with having to share my garden with snails as well as with being rejected for publications, no matter how hard I work on writing papers. Despite setbacks, the important thing is to always keep planting.

About the author

Liu Qian, from Chengdu City, Sichuan Province, is an Associate Professor at the School of Modern Languages and Cultures at the University of Warwick. Her research focuses on contemporary Chinese literature, comparative literature and translation studies. She holds a PhD from the University of Oxford and has previously taught at the School of Chinese Language and Literature at Beijing Normal University.

All Walks of Life

All the world's a stage,
And all the men and women merely players;
They have their exits and their entrances;
And one man in his time plays many parts.

William Shakespeare
As you Like It

Two Beggars

Written by: Qu Leilei
Translated by: Claire Xiong

"You must beg from everybody."

After developing a rapport with me, the beggar revealed the essence of his line of work. Although I was certain he hadn't read Dostoevsky, his words echoed a sentiment found in Dostoevsky's *The Insulted and Injured*.

That day, he sat by the street at the junction of Sloane Square and King's Road in central London, his eyes eagerly scanning the passersby.

"Excuse me, could you spare some change?" His hands, with long untrimmed nails, reached out as an old hat, containing a few coins, lay at his feet.

Seeing his lively appearance and sincere expression, I couldn't help but feel a sense of compassion, recalling my own days of poverty. With no pressing matters that day, I decided to sit down and chat with him.

I asked how I could help, and he confided that he didn't want to live like this but felt he had no other choice. He spoke of an organization in Cardiff, Wales, that helps people like him start anew. He wanted to go there but lacked the money for a train ticket.

As he spoke, tears welled up in his eyes. I gave him all the spare change I had and offered to draw a picture for him, mentioning that I am an artist. He told me that he once had dreams and hopes, but due to various reasons – familial, societal and personal – he lost everything. He had no home, no job, no friends – nothing left.

I didn't know how much of what he said was true, but my attentive listening must have touched him. As I was about to leave, I asked him to share some insights into the life of a beggar. Squinting one eye, he said, "You must beg from everyone."

This was my biggest takeaway that day – a profound insight into survival.

As a beggar, you never know who the giver will be. Well-dressed bosses and elegantly attired ladies often pass by without a glance, while ordinary people, tourists and children are the ones who drop a few coins into your old hat.

Some time later, I happened to pass by again. The beggar was still there, doing the same thing, telling the same stories to passersby. It seemed he hadn't gone to Wales after all. The picture I drew of him depicts him with one eye sincere and the other slightly cunning. As Gu Kaizhi, the celebrated painter of ancient China, said, "The spirit of a painting lies in the eyes."

I remembered the local government elections, where candidates from various parties knocked on doors, respectfully and warmly asking questions, then outlining their main policies, mostly on welfare, taxes and public safety, which are issues close to people's hearts, before asking for your vote. Regardless of their true intentions, they had to present themselves as the best caretakers of national and public interests. Those who win people's hearts win the world!

On a larger scale, it's just the same with the presidential election in the US and the Prime Minister election in the UK. "Vote for me, I'll cut taxes! Vote for me, I'll increase welfare! Vote for me, I'll improve employment, healthcare, education and public safety..."

It's all just the same, isn't it? Different professions, same nature. If you want to succeed, you must humble yourself and seek help from everyone, without distinction. This is what we call professionalism.

I once met another beggar, many years ago, shortly after I arrived in the UK. Apart from a roll of paintings and my two hands, I had nothing. I had to seize every opportunity to make money to survive before I could aspire to more.

At one point, I was invited to an arts festival in the southwest part of London. It was held in a large park filled with singers, dancers, glassblowers, painters, jugglers and food vendors – everything you could imagine. Such events are where people spend their small change, but I knew that small amounts could add up to something significant.

I quickly assessed the situation and started to make greeting cards, drawings of flowers and animals, small gifts, motto cards, and writing

Chinese names for British people combined with pictographic zodiac signs. People were happy to spend a few coins for a bit of fun, and it was a good chance for me to practise my calligraphy. Soon, a queue formed in front of me.

I earned quite a bit that day, filling my pockets with over two or three hundred pounds. The gleaming one-pound coins felt like gold to me, making me feel quite wealthy.

When the festival ended that evening, I tightened my belt to keep my heavily-loaded trousers from falling and pulled my cart of art supplies into the underground. Feeling happy, I silently made a vow to myself that I would help anyone in need that day.

Just then, I saw a beggar approaching from the far end of the platform. He was young, dishevelled and a bit dirty, holding out his hands for money. I reached into my pocket, ready to give him two or three of my golden pound coins. He stopped close to me and looked me up and down. And then, with a flick of his chin, he turned to ask someone else.

My first reaction was a surge of anger, "This one thinks he's too good for my money!" My second reaction was a bit of pity, "He didn't get any money, did he?" Probably no one was ever prepared to give him that much. Reflecting on it, I realised the reason: this is what we call amateurism.

To this day, I often think of these two beggars.

In recent years, many fresh postgraduates often seek my advice on how to start their next steps or venture into entrepreneurship. I have two key pieces of advice for them: first, be clear about what you want. Second, have a clear plan for how to achieve it. One is about the goal; the other is about the action.

About the author

Qu Leilei, originally from Beijing and born in the northeastern province of Heilongjiang, is the third son of Mr. Qu Bo, renowned Chinese writer, and Ms. Liu Bo. With a rich family heritage, he has delved into literature, history, philosophy and medicine. He began studying calligraphy and painting at the age of eight. In the summer of 1980, he co-founded the Stars Group with Ma Desheng, Huang Rui, and Zhong Acheng. In 1985, he moved to London. In 1999, he was elected President of the Chinese Painting and Calligraphy Association in the UK, Vice President of the Confederation of Chinese Associations UK, and trustee of the Chinese Arts Foundation in the UK. His works have won numerous international awards.

In Memory of Toby Eady

Written by: Wu Fan
Translated by: Chenlin Wang

I have mixed feelings about the United Kingdom. In my teenage years, the works of Dickens, Maugham, Woolf, Orwell and the Brontë sisters opened my eyes to the UK, and since then my bookshelf has gradually filled with the works of Kazuo Ishiguro, V.S. Naipaul, Ian McEwan and Julian Barnes. Although I had never been to the UK, I felt I learned quite a lot about the history, culture and people's daily life. I visited the UK three times later in my life, but to my embarrassment, each visit was brief. My real-life experiences in the UK are like the pieces of a jigsaw, rather than a scroll painting which depicts a continuous narrative. However, Toby Eady, my first literary agent, put those pieces together. The patterns depicted on these pieces by Toby have influenced my life, and always make me feel warm and grateful.

A few weeks ago, my British publisher invited me to meet my readers in the UK next summer for my new book, *Souls Left Behind*. Seven years were spent on this long historical novel, and it tells the story of 140,000 Chinese labourers recruited to Europe during World War I. The call with the publisher reminded me of Toby. I didn't have the chance to discuss this book with him before he passed, but I often thought of him during the writing process. He was the one who introduced me to the Western publishing world and encouraged me to listen to my inner voice when writing.

My first visit to England was nearly 20 years ago. At that time, I was looking for a literary agent for my first English novel. After years of working full-time at a high-tech company in Silicon Valley by day and staying up late to write at night, I was quite exhausted, but finding a literary agent was even more excruciating. In many Western countries, literary agents are known as the "gatekeepers of book publishing", and authors must secure a suitable agent to represent their works to publishers, which is, in writers' eyes, harder than finding a soulmate.

After nearly a year of seeking an agent in the US, I received nothing but rejections, mainly because my book was too "Chinese" to attract readers in the West. A few agents even suggested I make some changes to suit the Western market. As a last effort, I wrote an email to a small but renowned literary agency in the UK, introducing my novel and attaching the first three chapters. To my surprise, a few days later, I received a reply from Toby, the founder of this prestigious agency, asking why I was seeking an agent in the UK. I explained my reasons and sent him the electronic version of the entire manuscript as he requested. Although the seed of hope sprouted in my heart, I did not expect the flower to bloom. Writers know that even if a literary agent asks to read their entire manuscript, their decision is almost always a "no".

A few days later, my phone rang early in the morning at around five o'clock. Worried that something had happened to my parents or relatives in China, I jumped out of bed in a panic to answer the phone. I instinctively said "Hello" in Chinese as I picked up the phone. After a few seconds of silence, a slow, solemn voice with a thick British accent came from the other side. He said something, but my brain's language conversion function had not yet kicked in, so I was lost, thinking he might have dialled the wrong number. He continued to speak slowly, as if it were David Attenborough on the line. Then I understood – it was Toby! He said he had read my manuscript and loved it, and was inviting me to London to meet him as soon as possible. He always insisted on meeting the writer in person before deciding on representation. I asked my boss for leave, and a week later, I arrived in London, and stayed at the home of Toby and his wife Xinran.

I don't remember the weather or how the streets looked that day in London, but my first impression of Toby is clearly imprinted in my mind. He was the kind of scholarly, noble Englishman I had imagined (I later learned he indeed came from a noble family with ties to the royal family). He was in his early sixties at that time, tall and strong. His hair was silver, his steps were firm, and his words were delivered with grace and gravitas. Sometimes he would look into the distance with his sharp but kind eyes, as if spotting treasures unseen by others. His sneezes were forceful, and his laughter childlike. His home was elegant and full of charm, filled with books and artworks. A vase of fresh yellow daffodils was on the kitchen table, and on his bookshelves, I noticed the familiar works of many Chinese authors.

Shortly after I arrived, he started discussing my manuscript and the current state of literature in China and the West, asking me a series of questions. He mentioned not only his visits to China – his first visit in the 1970s, then several more since, but also Western publishing's misconceptions about China and the biases of Western readers. There was great passion and excitement in his voice. I was surprised that a person who did not know how to speak Chinese had such a deep love and understanding of China. A few hours later, I met his wife, Xinran, a renowned writer and senior media professional. We had a great chat, regretting not having met each other earlier, and I realised her significant influence on Toby. They were a rare pair of soulmates in the publishing world, a combination of Eastern and Western cultures.

Early the next morning, Toby got up. Seeing me unable to sleep due to jet lag, he invited me to take a walk in Hyde Park, which seemed to be his daily routine. Before leaving, he offered me a freshly baked croissant. As we made our way down the bustling streets of London, he walked confidently, hands behind his back, as if he were in a realm of his own. Pedestrians moved around him like water around a rock. If a mountain had blocked the way, I believe Toby would have cracked a tunnel with his presence. As the leaves swayed in the soft breeze, songbirds crafted an enchanting melody that danced through the air and Hyde Park's beauty regaled us in the background. But my attention was focused on my conversation with Toby. I was not used to his British accent, and his speech was peppered with many references, as if he were a professor. I would get lost if I zoned out. On top of that, I had to walk quickly to keep up with him. Before I knew it, we had reached the Serpentine. Seeing the swans swimming leisurely, he slowed down. A childlike smile spread across his face as he said, "Look at them, aren't they extraordinary?"

I returned to the US two days later to continue my day job, but my life was forever changed after meeting Toby. In just two weeks, he sold the English rights of my manuscript to publishing giant Macmillan, and secured rights in several other languages. A year later, with his help, my short story, *Year of the Monkey*, was published in the prestigious British literary magazine *Granta*, and another short story almost made it to *The New Yorker* (later published in *Ploughshares*).

My second visit to the UK was for the launch of my new book, *February Flowers*. Toby and Xinran hosted a celebration party at their home, where I met several British publishers, media people and writers. Before that party, I had attended reader events and literary festivals in Sydney, Melbourne, Singapore, Hong Kong and Beijing. At the party, Toby and Xinran always kept a watchful eye on the details. Seeing them flitting around the party, I was so grateful to have met such wonderful mentors and friends. I stayed in the UK for more than a week. Besides the party and reader events at bookstores, I toured some sights in London and the countryside with Toby and Xinran, which was a feast for my eyes and my mind.

Toby was an idealist. He represented many writers, including the famous bestselling author, Bernard Cornwell. Yet, he believed that representing ten good books in his lifetime was enough and that a writer should spend at least seven or eight years on one good piece of work. At the same time, he was a realist, understanding that for a writer to survive in the competitive, ever-changing publishing world, they needed to produce new works at least every three years, or even every one to two years. As one of the few Western literary agents representing Chinese writers, he had a profound understanding of the translation bottleneck and cultural dislocation between East and West. When I asked if he had any recommendations on what I should write about, he firmly said, "Listen to the call deep within your heart." When he was reading the first draft of my second novel, *Beautiful as Yesterday*, he often called me to discuss the historical background, plot and characters. Although sometimes he disagreed with my views, he always patiently listened to my explanations.

In the following years, I continued to be one of Toby's authors and assisted him and Xinran in promoting cultural exchanges between Chinese and Western publishing. I travelled with them to China multiple times. In the Chinese publishing world, people who were familiar with Toby called him "Da Tuo" (Big Toby in English). I still remember that autumn day when we visited Professor Feng Jicai at Tianjin University. As the rain continued its rhythmic patter, the leaves drifted downwards, their descent slow and almost hypnotic. Carried by the breeze, each one twirled, spiralled, and finally relinquished itself to the ground. Walking on the campus, Toby seemed lost in thought, gazing into the distance, speaking only a little, with his black coat billowing in the wind. The image of him standing with an air of quiet confidence stuck in my mind. Years later, when I learned he was battling an illness, I couldn't believe the bad news. He was the vibrant, passionate Toby! His sneezes could shake a room! How could he have cancer?

My third visit to the UK was in 2018. Toby had passed away on Christmas Eve a year earlier. Xinran picked me up at the train station. She looked frail and sad, with many new silver hairs on her head. Since Toby fell ill, she had been his secretary, nutritionist, and nurse. The next day, we went to his graveyard. He rested beneath the grass among the trees, with a black marble square tombstone embedded in the ground, carved with open book pages. On the left page, it reads: "Son of Mary Wesley and Heinz Ziegler/ Husband and soulmate of Xinran." On the right page, it reads: "Man of letters – Wise, Generous, Loyal." At the foot of the left page was a bouquet of yellow daffodils, and at the foot of the right page is a cute little bird perching on a branch. The tombstone was surrounded by white geraniums, daisies and pine cones. A gentle breeze blew, and a flock of small birds fluttered from the trees, soaring across the blue sky. Xinran often mentioned her spiritual connection with Toby. Among that flock of birds, could there be his reincarnation?

Dear Toby, shall we meet in the UK again next year?

About the author

Wu Fan, a Chinese-American bilingual writer, graduated from Sun Yat-sen University, and later studied at Stanford University. She is a volunteer and board member of MBL, and a founding member of the California-based nonprofit organisation Society of Heart's Delight (Yuyuanshe). Formerly employed at a high-tech company in Silicon Valley, she is now engaged in writing, book reviews and philanthropic work. Being translated into ten languages, and published in over twenty countries, her novels have been selected for the *TARGET BOOKMARK* and *San Francisco Chronicle*'s list of best books. Fan's latest book, *Souls Left Behind*, published by Huacheng Publishing House, was selected for the 2023 Annual List of Outstanding Chinese Literature in Taiwan, Hong Kong, Macao and Overseas.

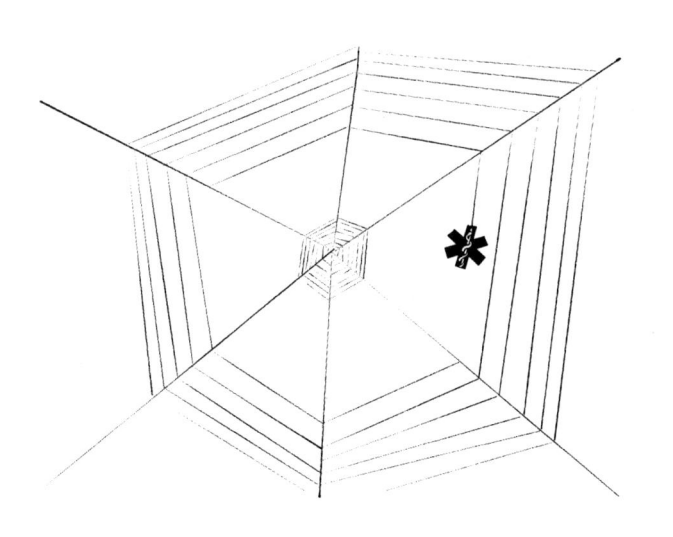

Experiencing COVID-19 in the UK

Written by: Yiwen
Translated by: Nyelin

The three years of the COVID-19 pandemic have been a global catastrophe, affecting everyone and every family. During that time, I was a resident doctor at a regional general hospital, witnessing firsthand the rise, peak and decline of the first wave of the pandemic in the UK. I personally treated countless patients and was among the first to be infected by the virus. Now, three years later, life has mostly returned to normal, and many memories have faded. Yet, the impact of COVID-19 lingers everywhere, and I often find myself reflecting on those experiences.

In early 2020, I was rotated to a district general hospital in southeast England for a six-month emergency internal medicine training. In the UK, apart from some major hospitals known as tertiary referral centres, most hospitals are smaller district general hospitals (DGH). This hospital was in a medium-sized town, not far from London, in a relatively affluent area. Many of the locals commuted to London for work, and many wealthy Londoners owned large houses here. The British Prime Minister's official retreat, Chequers, was nearby. A colleague once joked that if I stayed in the position of the emergency department, I might end up treating the Prime Minister. During the pandemic, that joke nearly came true, but that is another story.

1. The Storm Approaches

People who have lived in the UK for many years often feel that life here is very calm. Especially in rural areas, days go by quietly, with today seeming no different from yesterday. The emergence of a new virus in a faraway place seemed similarly remote. If someone told you this virus would affect everyone on the whole planet, you'd probably question their sanity. When I arrived at this hospital in February, Wuhan had already been locked down. The general sentiment in the UK was that this was just another "SARS", and China would control it. There was no sense of urgency. However, among the Chinese community, people were already taking action. Some friends began sending money and masks back to China. My younger daughter and a few of her friends took photos to show their support for China and Wuhan, hoping that the situation would improve.

As time passed, cases began to emerge across Europe and the United States. People realised that this virus was different from "SARS", and the control measures seemed ineffective. In early February, the hospital started posting notices at the entrance, "If you have a fever and have been to mainland China in the last two weeks, please do not enter the hospital. Please call 111." The hospital began requiring all staff to wear masks and assigned personnel to correct those who didn't wear them properly. The head of the infectious disease department is Chinese, and we chatted once during rounds. He said, "This virus seems to be a big problem and can't be eradicated. It will eventually reach the UK. Its societal impact could be as great as a world war." His words proved prophetic!

In March, Europe experienced widespread infections. The hospital began clearing wards to prepare for a large influx of patients. All inpatients who could go home were discharged, leaving the wards nearly empty, with only a handful of patients at most. One day, there were no patients at all, and we residents sat around chatting. Everyone felt lost and anxious and had no idea what was going to happen. That day, a resident who usually did extra shifts was worried about his income. Most people were more concerned about their health and that of their families, wondering whether they could survive this pandemic. The head of the respiratory department suddenly took on a much more prominent role, organising lectures on managing respiratory infections and emphasising the importance of conserving oxygen. The hospital also arranged mask fit tests for everyone to ensure their N95 masks were effective. Although the government promised a sufficient supply, in reality, N95 masks were scarce on the wards.

2. The First Case

One weekend in mid-to-late March, I was on duty. The previous day, a man in his sixties had been admitted with a fever and breathing difficulties. He had a recent travel history and underlying interstitial lung disease. A nasal swab had been taken, but the results would take three days. In the morning, the nurse told me his IV line was blocked and needed replacing. I was about to draw blood, so I prepared the necessary items and went to see him. He was in a single room, but since he wasn't a confirmed COVID patient yet, I couldn't wear an N95 mask or protective clothing. So I only wore a regular surgical mask. He was lying in the bed with a high-flow oxygen nasal cannula, breathing 60 litres per minute, but in good spirits. He chatted with me while I worked. He was British, and had travelled extensively in Asia. He lived in Thailand and Malaysia for twenty to thirty years. Now, since he was older and less mobile, he had returned to the UK. He spoke fondly of Asian food and the climate of Southeast Asia. He had no family, but his brother lived nearby. He said he had no clean clothes and his brother was bringing him some. Everything went smoothly. I inserted a catheter, drew some blood. After saying goodbye to him, I went on to deal with other matters.

Two hours later, the nurse urgently called me, saying the patient's oxygen saturation had dropped to the 80s. I rushed over and found it was true. He was at 83%. He was clearly in respiratory distress and already unconscious. The situation was dire so I immediately called a nurse to activate the emergency rescue mechanism and bring in the emergency team, while also summoning the attending physician. The attending physician arrived within minutes and quickly went in to see the patient. The emergency team arrived shortly after. After I briefed them on the situation, the team leader said, "The patient is high-risk; we must take protective measures." They then methodically donned protective gowns, face shields and goggles according to the protocol. I stood there, watching them staying calm and collected, feeling like I was waiting for an eternity! Of course, I knew they were doing the right thing. Staying busy but orderly maximised our chances of executing a high-quality resuscitation. After they went in, I stayed outside the door relaying messages, passing samples, and reading lab reports for them. They worked tirelessly, performing CPR, inserting arterial lines, administering external defibrillation, and so on. But the patient showed no signs of improvement. Eventually, he was pronounced dead.

Afterwards, the emergency team and the on-site staff held a short meeting in the adjacent office. This was the first case of suspected COVID-19 at our hospital. The team leader summarised the procedures and shortcomings, then warned everyone to self-isolate and report to the hospital immediately if they developed a fever within the next few days. As I escorted them out of the ward, a middle-aged man was standing just outside the corridor, holding a bag, saying he had brought clothes for his brother. His brother was the patient. Clearly, he was still unaware of what had happened. I reported this to the attending physician, who then went to inform the patient's family.

This was our hospital's first suspected COVID-19 death. Just a few hours before he passed, the patient had been joking and chatting with me. Now he was gone. When I returned to the ward, I saw the nurse in charge of the patient crying, and the Chief of Respirology was there comforting her. The Chief was usually very strict and rarely smiled. It was unusual to see her showing emotion. Later, the patient's test results came out: COVID-19 positive.

3. "Hitting the Mark"

After returning home, I told my family about what had happened and immediately decided to write a will. Living in the UK, it makes sense to have a will in place early. A friend of mine shared his experience when his partner passed away without a will. He had to endure the pain of losing his loved one while also spending money and effort on various legal documents. He advised me to take care of it early. However, with the complexities of work and life, finding the time to handle this long-overdue task was never easy. Now, it seemed like the perfect opportunity.

The next day, I was off, so I had two friends witness and sign the will.

When making it, I couldn't help but feel a bit like a warrior setting off on a perilous journey.

On the third day, I went back to work. After doing my rounds, I went to review medical records and suddenly felt a bit off. I experienced a moment of dizziness and was unsteady on my feet. After a few more unsteady steps, the same feeling returned. A nurse was checking a patient's temperature, so I borrowed her thermometer and took my own temperature: 37.6°C! The hospital had issued a notice a few days earlier stating that if anyone developed a fever, they must stop working immediately and go into isolation. I quickly informed my colleagues, and then drove home.

Upon arriving home, I notified the hospital's occupational health department and was instructed to isolate for seven days. I asked if I could get a throat swab test and they said no, as testing kits were limited and only hospitalised critical cases could be tested. That day, I moved myself into the small study downstairs, using the downstairs bathroom exclusively. My husband left meals at the door in disposable containers, and I took out the rubbish after a few days.

My children were not allowed to enter my room and could only talk to me through the door, which made them quite unhappy. My youngest daughter, who loves hugs and close contact, was especially upset. Her older sister was away at college and couldn't visit often. Now, with her father isolated in a small room, she was very unhappy.

In the next two or three days, my symptoms worsened. I felt light-headed, had body aches, and was completely exhausted. I spent the entire day resting in bed. The small study, only about two or three square metres large, had a small desk and a single bed. When I was awake, there was little to do, and I often watched the spider on the wall busily spinning its web. It made me think of the story of Robert the Bruce, the King of Scotland, who was inspired by a spider to persevere and eventually reclaim his throne. I wondered if I would have a chance for my own "comeback".

Various thoughts kept swirling in my mind. With the will taken care of, I no longer worried about that. Instead, I reflected on my life – my growth, education and career. After graduating from medical school, I decided to pursue research. I completed my master's and PhD before leaving mainland China. After many years of research, I returned to clinical practice. And now, I faced COVID-19. I worried what would happen to my family if things got bad. I also felt anxious, fearing that I might have already infected my family and friends before showing symptoms. Yet, I held onto a bit of hope, thinking, "I can't be that unlucky, can I?"

During those days, my daughter could occasionally talk to me from the outside of the door. Sometimes she sang. It was the only comfort I had during that time! By the fourth day, my condition began to improve. The fever subsided and my appetite slowly returned. A week later, I had fully recovered and returned to work. Neither my family nor the friends who helped me with the will showed any symptoms. From that moment on, I decided to designate the small study as a semi-contaminated area in our home. Every day after returning from work, the first thing I did was to go to the small study to change my clothes. Only after showering could I give my daughter a big hug.

Because I hadn't undergone a throat swab test, I was never officially diagnosed. Later, the hospital allowed healthcare workers to test each other for COVID-19 antibodies, so I asked a colleague to draw blood for me. The next day, the result came out. I was positive for antibodies, confirming that I had indeed been infected with COVID-19.

4. The Rise and Fall

A few days later, the UK started a nationwide lockdown. The route I took to work was a major artery leading to London, usually bustling with traffic. Now, there was only me on the wide four-lane road. Supermarkets started experiencing panic-buying. When healthcare workers finished their shifts, they often found the shelves empty. A nurse tearfully posted a video saying she couldn't buy food. After the video aired on TV, major supermarkets began opening special sessions for healthcare workers. I went once, standing in a long, winding queue, braving the cold wind. Fortunately, the government quickly designated supermarket staff and truck drivers as key workers, allowing them to work during the lockdown, and the supermarket supply situation began to improve. Later on, the Prime Minister was admitted to intensive care. He fell ill while residing in Downing Street, not at Chequers, so he was taken to St. Thomas' Hospital in London, narrowly missing being admitted to the hospital where I worked.

The atmosphere in the hospital was becoming increasingly tense, as all efforts were directed towards preparing for the impending COVID-19 surge. Non-COVID patients were becoming rare sightings, and those few who were admitted eventually tested positive. To reduce in-hospital infections, healthcare workers started wearing isolation gowns, which quickly became scarce. The emergency department was particularly unhappy, as staff from other departments would "steal" their gowns. Eventually, the hospital distributed gowns to all doctors. Female doctors wore red isolation gowns, which looked quite nice, while male doctors wore brown ones, prompting some to joke that they resembled the colour of faeces. Shift handovers also became problematic. Initially, attempts were made to conduct handovers in outdoor spaces, but this was discontinued after two days. It compromised patient privacy and no one could endure standing in the cold wind for half an hour at 10 p.m. After weighing the pros and cons, the hospital designated the largest room available and mandated that everyone wear masks during handovers. While it couldn't guarantee a two-metre safety distance between individuals, it was a stark departure from the previous crowded handover situations.

Later on, the hospital became a hotspot for infections, with more and more healthcare workers infected with COVID-19. There were constant reports of doctors and nurses from various departments being admitted to the intensive care unit. Eventually, one nurse who was infected with the virus passed away despite rescue efforts. He was a Filipino, in the prime of his life, leaving behind a wife and children. On the day of his burial, his hearse slowly circled the hospital building, and all staff who could attend came out to bid him farewell, many with tears streaming down their faces. In our department, a nurse manager also ended up in the ICU, but fortunately, she later recovered. Everyone felt the spectre of death looming not far away.

In May, the situation began to improve, and the tide of the pandemic gradually receded. COVID-19 cases decreased, while the case rates of other patients started to increase. Our training slowly returned to normal. Afterwards, I applied for training as a general practitioner (GP) and was successfully accepted into a programme close to home. In early August, I bid farewell to this hospital and started the new position.

Someone says that in the grand sweep of time, each person is like a grain of sand, seemingly insignificant. COVID-19 has made everyone realise the fragility of life. Amid the pandemic, I witnessed countless farewells between loved ones, felt the anxiety and helplessness of patients' families numerous times over the phone, and saw desperation and helplessness in the eyes of patients. Many times, I questioned the value of my work as a doctor. Witnessing the passing of so many vibrant lives truly makes one cherish everything that they have, every minute spent with family, and every "luxury" they have in life – the most important of which is good health.

About the author

Yiwen graduated from a medical school in China and holds a PhD in immunology. He has been engaged in scientific research at the University of Oxford for many years and is currently working as a general practitioner (GP).

A Chance Encounter with Giuseppe Eskenazi

Written by: Cai Fang
Translated by: Rebecca Zhang

Giuseppe Eskenazi, a globally renowned authority and a leading collector of Asian antiques, made headlines in July 2005. At a Christie's auction in London, he acquired the Yuan dynasty blue and white porcelain jar featuring the "Guiguzi Descending the Mountain" design for an astounding £15.688 million (approximately RMB 230 million). This purchase set a world record for the price of Chinese artifacts and remains the highest price ever paid for Chinese porcelain. This milestone purchase marks an indelible contribution to the global recognition of Chinese art.

It was said to be a "chance encounter", but in truth, I had come to meet him. I had a premonition that I would meet Mr. Eskenazi because it was known that he often spent his time at his art gallery at 10 Clifford Street in London. On the day I visited, the gallery was hosting its 50th-anniversary special exhibition. The morning after the exhibition opened, my friend Yan and I visited the gallery, which is located in a bustling area of London, next to Sotheby's and Bonhams auction houses. As the three-storey building came into view, a white flag with blue and green lettering reading "ESKENAZI" fluttered at the entrance, with the exhibition dates printed on the glass window. A large poster of the "Guiguzi Descending the Mountain" scroll hung inside the gallery, clearly visible from across the street.

I peered inside the window while Yan eagerly made her way to the entrance. I held her back, as I panicked with excitement. "Wait. Let me think about what to say. What if Eskenazi is inside? How should I express my admiration for him...?" Before I could finish my thought, the door opened. "Please come in," said an elderly man. "Mr. Eskenazi! It's you, isn't it?" I recognised the man who opened the door with excitement, the one known as the "Godfather of Chinese Porcelain". He smiled and pointed inside the gallery, "The porcelain you want to see is inside. Please go ahead."

"Could we take a photo with you first? Meeting you is so exciting for me." I eagerly asked, showing more interest in him than the superlative porcelain jar. He shook his head and said, "No, no photos," then pointed inside again. We didn't press further and walked in to view the exhibition of the "Four Perfect Porcelains and One Jade", renowned for their delicate beauty. Although I was disappointed about not getting the chance to introduce myself and I felt somewhat out of place wearing my fieldwork shoes from my doctoral studies, the "Guiguzi" was dazzling. The exquisite composition, the rich cobalt hues and the delicate and lively brushwork were exactly as I had imagined. The jar was larger than I had expected. In fact, all the Yuan dynasty porcelain pieces I saw were larger than predicted. The large size catered to the needs of the Yuan dynasty Mongols who travelled extensively on horseback and reflected the advancements in porcelain-making techniques of the time, as well as the flourishing overseas trade. According to the Ming dynasty's *The Overall Survey of the Ocean's Shores*, the people of Java "had no beds or stools, nor spoons or chopsticks for eating", and during meals, "they would sit around and have a dish well-filled with rice which they moisten with butter and gravy; and in eating they use the hand to take up the food and place it in the mouth." No wonder they "loved Chinese blue and white porcelain the most"; the large plates and jars exported to the Western Regions were perfectly compatible with the local custom of eating communally.

Yan and I took numerous photos and videos of the porcelain jar, reverently admiring its details, but also sneaking in a few coy selfies. As we snapped, we were the only visitors in the gallery. I noticed an introduction about the jar on the wall and went over to read it. The description, accompanied by illustrations, stated that the jar was made during the Yuan dynasty and was 27.5 cm high. One illustration showed a side of the jar with the "Guiguzi" design, and the other was a print from which the design was inspired.

The English text read:

"This unique jar is a representative work of Yuan dynasty blue and white porcelain, one of the few narrative scene depictions of the time. The imagery often originated from printed illustrations. This jar depicts the historical story of the sage Guiguzi descending the mountain to rescue his student Sun Bin. Guiguzi is shown majestically sitting on a one-seat chariot pulled by two feline animals. The scene illustrates his meeting with the Qi state envoy Su Dai, who rides a spotted horse and comes to seek Guiguzi's help. Similar compositions appear in illustrations from the 1320s. The Mongol rulers' support for woodblock printing led to the revival of this industry, resulting in flourishing centers in Jian'an, Fujian. Clearly, workers at the nearby Jingdezhen kilns had access to these illustrations."

After reading, I had questions about two phrases, so I called out to Mr. Eskenazi. I asked, "Mr. Eskenazi, may I ask you a question?" He stopped and nodded, indicating he was willing to answer.

"I'm not sure if 'feline animals' is the correct term. In Yuan dynasty texts and illustrations, they are referred to as 'two tigers', but the jar depicts a tiger and a leopard. I would suggest 'two beasts' instead. What do you think?"

"Yes, the imagery differs from the text," he said. "This jar was loaned to the Shanghai Museum for six months in 2012-2013, and we discussed this topic then. We agreed that the term was acceptable."

I continued, "And about the term 'meeting', I don't think this depicts the meeting scene between Guiguzi and Su Dai. Based on the composition and their body language, it seems they are descending the mountain together after meeting, with Su Dai following on horseback. A meeting scene would likely show them face-to-face. What do you think?"

"You must understand that Chinese porcelain is unique, and Chinese painting techniques are subtle and indirect," he said. "The lack of a face-to-face depiction doesn't mean it's not a meeting scene."

"I know, I studied this in my doctoral thesis which compared Chinese porcelain with Greek vase painting," I asserted. "The latter is more direct. But here, it's not about subtlety; the chariot is heading downhill, indicating they have already met."

"How can you compare Chinese porcelain with Greek vases? Chinese porcelain is unique," he said, agitated.

I smiled disarmingly and replied, "I didn't explain clearly. I'm comparing their storytelling methods, not their craftsmanship or other aspects. I'm focused on the narratives depicted in the imagery. I've collected over 200 story illustrations from Chinese porcelain. 'Guiguzi Descending the Mountain' is a significant one."

He sighed in relief. "Oh, that makes sense. Chinese porcelain is unique, incomparable to anything else. A few years ago, a PhD student from a Chinese university argued that the chariot on the jar should be depicted going uphill, not downhill. I disagreed with him."

"Uphill?" I questioned. "That doesn't make sense. Whether meeting Su Dai or rescuing his student, Guiguzi would never be heading uphill."

He nodded, "Exactly. That's why I disagreed. And you know, Chinese philosophy emphasises…"

I interjected. "Chinese philosophy emphasises humility. Guiguzi's seated posture and the chariot facing downhill embody this humility. Chinese people often name their study rooms 'Half-Moon Cabin' or 'So-and-so Cottage' because full moon implies fullness which is not conducive to…"

I couldn't find the right words to express "humility brings benefit, arrogance invites loss".

"Not conducive to practise asceticism," he said. "Chinese culture values the 'Golden Mean'." I was pleased to see his deep understanding of Chinese culture and said, "I hope you'll remember one day that another PhD student from China said this is not a scene of Guiguzi meeting Su Dai."

He nodded and said, "Yes, it's not a meeting scene. It should be them descending the mountain after their meeting."

I was delighted that he agreed with my interpretation. Yan seized the moment and asked, "Can we take a photo with you?" This time, he obliged.

Mr. Eskenazi came from a family of antique dealers and had given up his medical career to take over the gallery from his father. The business had been in the family for three generations, and his son was now taking it over from him. Despite being in his 80s and a bit unsteady on his feet, he personally greeted all visitors at the door, gave them ample space to appreciate the collection and made himself available to answer questions. Through his demeanor and actions, I felt his reverence for Chinese art.

Before leaving, Yan and I purchased two copies of a catalogue that was printed especially for the exhibition. As I ran my fingers over its glossy pages, I realized that Mr. Eskenazi was like the porcelain itself gentle yet resilient, transparent and crystalline with a delicate glass glaze; bright as a mirror and resonant as a chime.

About the author

Cai Fang is an Associate Professor at the School of Foreign Languages, Jiangxi Normal University; and a visiting scholar in the Department of English at the University of Cambridge.

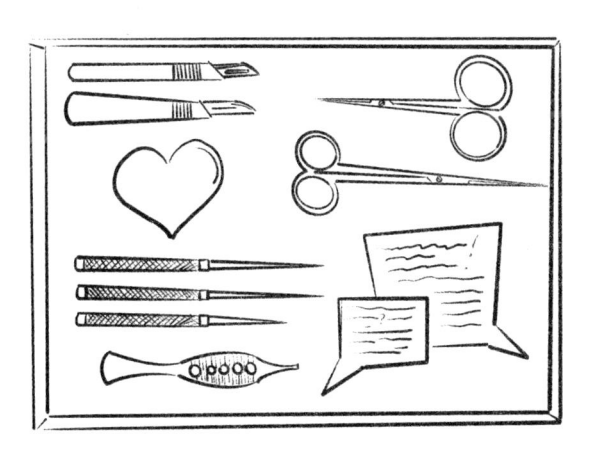

My Days in the Plastic Surgery Department

Written by: Wang Li
Translated by: Camila Tay

In my five years in the plastic surgery department, I've experienced a range of emotions – joy, anger, worry, sadness and fear. I'm immensely grateful for this experience, which I hold dear. Though I've never undergone plastic surgery, I feel like the experience of working in the field has made me a completely different person, inside and out.

1. Background

Medical professionals are often portrayed on TV as quick on their feet, with nurses instinctively handing over surgical tools with just a glance from the surgeon. I've always admired this seamless coordination. My fascination grew while watching the TV series *Qi Ren Qi An* (translated as "Strange People, Strange Cases"), particularly the chemistry between the medical student, played by Carman Lee, and the handsome doctor.

Driven by curiosity and admiration, I pursued a career in surgery, eventually landing a job in the Plastic Surgery department at the West Wing of John Radcliffe Hospital in Oxford. The department originally began as the Radcliffe Infirmary (RI), Oxford's first hospital, which opened in 1770. The RI has a rich history, including serving as a military hospital during WWI and being the site where the first dose of penicillin was injected into a human patient. When the RI closed in 2007, the department moved to the newly constructed West Wing, which now boasts world-class facilities in neurosurgery, plastic surgery, pediatrics, ophthalmology and ENT.

The move from RI was controversial, with many senior employees opposing it and even resigning. Some referred to the new facility as "JR2", which they likened to the humiliation of the Jingkang Incident in Chinese history, which involved the siege, fall and sacking of the Song capital city of Kaifeng in imperial China as well as the abduction and relegation of the dynasty's emperor Qinzong. Even years later, colleagues frequently reminisced about the RI, and I often felt a pang of sadness for not having been part of that chapter.

After making it through the interview, background check and physical examination, I started my new job on November 2nd. I vividly remember walking through the autumn leaves, feeling both anxious and excited. A middle-aged man commented on my determined footsteps, which I initially took as a compliment, though I now suspect he was being sarcastic because my loud footsteps likely disturbed him.

At the hospital, I was greeted by K, the head nurse of the plastic surgery department, who introduced me to the team. My first impression of the operating room was one of awe – it was far more spacious and bright than what I had seen during my internship at a hospital in Beijing. The facility had three distinct rooms: the anesthetic room, the preparation room, and the disposal room. K explained that our department focused not on cosmetic surgery but on reconstructive procedures for conditions like craniofacial deformities, cleft lips, hand deformities, mastectomies and trauma repairs. She proudly said: "Our team offers treatment for patients from head to toe. It will be a great learning experience and you will have plenty of opportunities to develop your skills, but of course, we will be very busy." With that, a journey filled with challenges and discovery began.

2. Facing off against "bossy" superiors

As a newcomer, I underwent a six-month training programme, including three months of classes and three months of rotations. My first major surgery was a mastectomy with free flap reconstruction. In this procedure, one of the patient's breasts is removed, and a section of muscle from around the navel area is used to reconstruct a breast. The advantage of this surgery is that the patient ends up with a perfect breast and a flat abdomen, killing two birds with one stone.

The chief surgeon, known for his temper, made me nervous even before the surgery began. Despite my best efforts, I made a mistake during the operation, and the surgeon responded angrily. "Give me your hand," he said, before slapping the instrument into it. I was feeling both scared and angry, so I followed his instructions and slammed the vascular clamp onto his hand. Perhaps I had used too much force, as the tool came loose the moment it reached the chief surgeon. He looked at me with a deadly glare.

As a shy and inexperienced newbie, I often felt bullied by my colleagues, and the thought of working with this aggressive surgeon caused me many sleepless nights. Yet I refused to quit, telling myself, "I love this job. I will not leave because of anyone."

Over time, I realised that the surgeon's anger stemmed from the stress and complexity of the surgeries. He might have expected more support from me and was frustrated by my inexperience. As the Chinese saying goes, he might have "hated the iron for not becoming steel", which means to feel resentful towards someone for failing to meet expectations and impatient to see improvement.

Recognising the need for better communication, I devised a strategy to take the initiative in the operating room. During our next surgery, I kept the circulating nurse informed and even instructed her to fetch additional tools when needed. To my surprise, the surgeon remained calm throughout, and later specifically requested me to assist him in future surgeries. During one operation, I noticed he was struggling to cut a particular tissue. Before he could lose his temper, I decided that I should step in to do something, and loudly instructed the circulating nurse to grab a new pair of surgical scissors. When she told me that there were none left, I responded even more loudly, "If there are none, you can borrow them from another department, or even from another hospital." The circulating nurse began to giggle and signalled to me that I was overacting. Meanwhile, the overbearing surgeon responded calmly that he would just work with that pair of scissors.

Working with this surgeon made me realise the importance of communication. Raised in China, I was taught to be humble and keep a low-profile. I assumed that "speaking less and doing more" was the optimal approach in everything. However, it appeared that especially outside of China, "speaking less" could sometimes lead one to being seen as a "sick cat", a Chinese term that means a weak person. In this context, being humble could lead to one being perceived as lacking confidence, and it is important to actively express oneself.

3. Interacting with passive bosses

Not all surgeons are overbearing. I once assisted Alex, a British surgeon with Australian training, known for his easygoing nature and love for playing pop songs during surgery – I have him to thank for introducing me to my first Taylor Swift song. During the end of a muscle transplant surgery for a young patient who had been in a car accident, I was taking account of all the medical instruments and noticed something missing. It seemed like the green film that is placed under the blood vessels to give the surgeon a clearer view for suturing could have been left inside the patient's wound. When I alerted Alex, he calmly thanked me, and we re-opened the leg to check. He removed the fingernail-sized film without issue, and reassured me that while the mistake wouldn't have harmed the patient significantly, it would have weighed heavily on our conscience.

After hearing this, I felt extremely touched. How did he understand my inner thoughts so well? I knew that he believed I was an upright person, and I would always live in guilt if I made a mistake. His affirmation gave me immense strength. Any time I face a similar situation that leaves me conflicted, I ask myself, "If I do this, will I be able to sleep soundly for the rest of my life?" This is probably why I particularly love the phrase, "No guilt in life, no fear in death" – my lifelong pursuit.

4. The "tall, rich and handsome" doctor and the damsel in distress

This story happened over a decade ago, yet it remains a classic memory often shared during gatherings with current and former colleagues. At that time, I was Dr. Adam's scrub nurse. Dr. Adam, a young and witty chief surgeon, exuded sophistication while maintaining a low profile. Known as the "tall, rich and handsome" doctor, he had a fan-base of nurses across all ages and departments.

I was about two months pregnant then, though none of my colleagues knew. One morning, after preparing the medical instruments, I suddenly felt dizzy, my vision darkened, and I whispered, "I'm about to faint." Dr. Adam, who was standing behind me, quickly supported me and gently laid me down on the ground. As I lay there with my vision completely gone, I could hear his calm voice urging me to move my legs gently. He asked, "Did you add sugar to your tea this morning?" I replied, "No." Then, he inquired if I was on my period. Quietly, I told him, "I'm pregnant." With the enthusiasm of announcing good news, he exclaimed, "Well done!"

My eyes flew open in shock. Initially, I did not plan on announcing my pregnancy in such a way, but it was too late. The department head and a few colleagues rushed over upon hearing the news. The situation felt incredibly awkward, and I wished I could disappear. As a colleague escorted me to the sick bay, the first thing she asked was, "Why didn't you stay on the ground longer? You missed such a good opportunity." She jokingly added that if she had fainted, she would have told Dr. Adam she couldn't breathe. I laughed and replied, "That wouldn't work – there's a respirator right there; why would Dr. Adam be needed?"

After fainting during my shift as Dr. Adam's scrub nurse, I was "forced" to go home and rest. I told my supervisor, "I'm fine, I can keep working. I just have a little low blood pressure." I'll never forget her reply, "I'm not just responsible for you; I'm responsible for the patient too. Someone who doesn't have enough blood flowing in their veins can't serve others." Her words were logical, clear and compelling. I later found myself using the same reasoning when advising colleagues and friends. At that time, I was focused on working hard, but her words enlightened me – I realised that resting was the better way to be responsible to the patients. When I got home, I lay down with determination, reminding myself, "Only by taking care of yourself can you take care of others." My mother had often told me this, and it turns out she was right.

These stories are just a few of the unforgettable moments from my time in the plastic surgery department. Countless more memories, though they fade with time, still spring to mind unexpectedly, transforming into a magical force that inspires and empowers me to face life positively.

The National Health Service (NHS) in the UK is full of talented individuals with interesting and compassionate souls. Perhaps it is because everyone has an understanding and acceptance of mortality that they embrace life with more respect and a lighter heart. It was common to hear in my department that we need to treat our patients as if they are our family.

For example, a doctor who performed cleft lip surgeries for children always used the smallest surgical needles to stitch the lips of the young patients. He explained, "Lips are extremely important to girls. The quality of the stitching will directly impact her first kiss in the future." Another doctor who performed head and neck surgeries would always say a little prayer while cleaning a patient's wound after a tumour removal. As he poured the saline on the patient's wound, he would chant, "Die, cancer, die!" Every time I heard this, a quote from one of John Green's novels would come to me, "The world is not a wish granting factory."

To me, the relationship between patients and medical staff is one of mutual healing. We care for their illnesses, while they remind us to cherish our loved ones and appreciate the blessing of good health.

About the author

Wang Li, a registered nurse in the UK, joined Oxford University Hospitals in 2008. She worked as an instrument nurse in plastic surgery for five years before transitioning to an anesthesia nurse role. She is currently a Senior Specialist Nurse in Preoperative Assessment. She loves life and work and enjoys recording and sharing interesting stories from her life.

Survive or Perish: Learning to Thrive

Written by: Zimin
Translated by: Yan Jun

The last time I attended a company training with colleagues, I shared how I managed to arrive on time despite facing numerous challenges. They were concerned about my lack of work-life balance, and kindly arranged a taxi for me to go home after the training was complete. I've always been hesitant to trouble others, so their kindness deeply moved me. "You deserve it," they said. "We'll get you here in a limo from now on. You're wonderful and deserve to be looked after!" Their words warmed my heart like a fire in winter. I was reminded of the people I've met and the experiences I've had over the years. Suddenly, I realised that being a good person is indeed rewarding, and facing life's challenges with unwavering kindness is the best approach.

1. At the edge

Before and after the pandemic, we endured several years of hardship. The competition in scientific research was fierce and countless CVs were sent out with no response. Oxford, though small, is a place teeming with hidden talent. Many PhDs and postdocs vie for even the most obscure jobs, with positions at Oxford University being the most competitive, often already decided or requiring funding to join a group.

For someone like me – middle-aged, introverted and somewhat socially anxious – the job hunt was disheartening. I doubted my choices in the first half of my life, feeling like I was walking a tightrope only to find I was heading in the wrong direction. At the brink of despair, a classmate in the US suggested I switch professions and explore a career in medical device registration and access. So, I bought a thick professional book and painstakingly worked through it bit by bit. Eventually, I finished it. From that moment, the gears of fate began to turn, and my life embarked on a new journey.

I first joined a Software as a Medical Device (SaMD) company in Oxford, where I was responsible for registering access to SaMD products. This was a significant challenge for me, given my lack of a computing background, and I worried about how I would get along with my younger colleagues, who were ten or twenty years younger than me. I didn't know much about their interests and wasn't particularly interested in the topics they discussed. Fortunately, my boss had organised a cake day every Thursday, where the access, quality and clinical teams took turns bringing cakes to the office, allowing us to eat and chat. I love baking, and I conquered their "stomachs" with just two cakes, gradually becoming more acquainted with my colleagues through "cake diplomacy".

Over the course of a year, I started developing and registering new software medical device products, as well as modifications to existing products. I often took on the most challenging tasks in the group. As the days and months passed, I gradually became a go-to consultant within the group and across departments in the company. When I was about to leave, my colleagues gave me a small owl accessory, jokingly calling me the "wise one". On my last day at the office, my boss made a cake for me, and his sincerity touched my heart. Exchanging sincerity for sincerity and earning the respect of others through hard work is the true joy on life's journey.

2. Mind the gap

I have a particularly capable classmate named Lu. Years ago, when he saw that I had been working at the same company for four or five years, he said, "You should regularly put yourself on the job market to test the waters." At first, I didn't take his advice to heart. It wasn't until 2021 that I realised the wisdom in his words – I should have been applying for more jobs, building a network in my field, and staying in touch with headhunters.

In the summer of 2022, I did six or seven interviews and received two job offers: one from an in-vitro testing company and another from a pharmaceutical registration access consulting firm, both offering similar salaries and benefits. I was torn because I had heard many complaints about the high stress levels at consulting firms. The headhunters from both sides tried hard to persuade me to join their respective companies. When I talked to Lu, he said, "You're such a strong learner; what are you afraid of? It's no fun to always play it safe, and you'll be working for many years to come." I replied, "I'm too gentle, somewhat socially anxious, and a foreigner." Lu responded confidently, "I'm also an introvert. Life forces everyone to step up when needed!"

It's been almost a year since I joined the consulting firm as a novice. Reflecting on this year's journey, filled with ups and downs, I sometimes wonder how I managed to get through it. Unlike the relatively homogeneous cultural background of the software company, my colleagues and clients at the consulting firm come from all over the world, with vastly different educational backgrounds and work experiences. Most of my colleagues are experts with ten or twenty years of experience, having been "poached" from major pharmaceutical companies or government drug approval departments. During client meetings, they often humorously highlight their extensive experience in the self-introduction sessions. In comparison, my qualifications seem insignificant, so I focus on relevant experience to meet clients' needs. Sometimes I joke with colleagues that I am the "junior" senior consultant. When I have to handle various questions from six or seven senior executives of a client company, an hour of straightforward Q&A feels like a battle.

Consulting companies differ from industrial companies in that, besides reporting to your boss, you need to communicate and collaborate with multiple stakeholders both internally and externally. The hardest part is working remotely from home, where you must proactively communicate and plan for many issues. The most important lesson I learned during my year in the consulting firm is that my approach to problems and perspectives has evolved. I learned how to ask the right questions, how to ask good questions, and how to guide clients step-by-step in solving their difficulties. Another crucial aspect of my growth is learning how to manage expectations:

>   What can I accomplish on my own?
>   What requires help from the team?
>   What needs to be negotiated with the client?

When consulting internally with colleagues, you need to consider their time, and if their time cannot be billed to the current project, you need to promptly discuss any potential issues upfront.

3. Dare to say no

As the only Chinese person in the company and a newcomer, my first priority was to survive the new challenges before considering long-term development. Over the past year, no matter how daunting the tasks assigned by my boss were, I never said "no". I understood that as a newcomer, I needed to gain as much practical experience as possible, and dealing with clients' issues has helped me grasp the complexities of regulations in practice. The downside is that I had to endure a war of attrition, grappling with the ever-evolving regulations from the US, Europe, the UK and other countries. One colleague jokingly remarked, "Go home, have a baby, and come back to find you've lost track of the new regulations." The regulatory access industry truly requires constant learning and improvement; it's a never-ending journey of growth.

Mid-year, when I travelled to Belgium with the company's senior consultant to provide training to clients, I was captivated by her mannerisms and professionalism. When clients asked questions, she sometimes responded, "I don't know the answer to that question; no one knows the answer." While this is sometimes true, I never had the courage to answer a question that way, thinking that clients expect definitive answers when they pay for a consultation. Answering these types of questions with the right attitude and tone of voice is a technical skill that requires experience. Over time, I noticed that many of my older and more experienced colleagues also had questions they didn't know the answers to and sometimes sought help in our group chat. It became clear that not knowing everything is normal. Additionally, my colleagues encouraged me to practise the art of negotiation to my advantage. Even if you don't say "no", you can still strive to secure as many resources as possible to make your work easier and more efficient.

4. A tale of two cities

This year, many consulting firms are merging, blending traditional registration and approval consultancies with capital to chase quick, substantial profits. Our company was merged two months ago, and integrating two completely different styles has been challenging. The company we merged with operates freely and in an improvisational way, while we prefer a systematic approach. They frequently hold brainstorming meetings, whereas we nearly complete our reports on the first draft.

Our two companies barely overlap in consulting areas. They are more up-to-date, using flashy PowerPoint presentations, mind maps, and various types of assistive software. Initially, we thought Teams and Zoom were sufficient for daily communication, but now we are asked to use Slack, Jira, and other tools, which has sparked many complaints. Our veteran consultants wonder why something that could be explained in a few sentences has to be made so complicated. Tools should support the work; if not used properly, they become a hindrance. As the saying goes, "It's like putting socks on a rooster".

Despite these challenges, the merger offers significant benefits, especially for individuals. It provides greater exposure to the entire business life cycle–from product development to market launch and subsequent marketing and sales. Understanding and implementing strategies across these stages is invaluable. The same insights would cost hundreds of thousands of dollars at a business school. Life isn't static; we must constantly seek our optimal "hit" point, re-enter the turbulence and find a new balance.

5. Stay true

Unlike my last company, where I used cake as an icebreaker, it's been challenging to have in-depth conversations with my colleagues since I work 100 percent remotely. The company organises face-to-face dinners and training events once or twice a year, providing rare opportunities to get to know each other better. Around the dinner table and at the bar, we share gossip and personal stories, and a few glasses of wine later, the conversation flows freely. One colleague's catchphrase is "long story short"; you think his story is ending, but it leads into a sequel, only for him to say "long story short" again. The drinking culture in the UK is a bit different from that in China, but the effect is the same – working together and then socializing definitely accelerates the process of becoming close-knit, like a gang.

Because I love taking photos, I often capture funny moments when everyone is together. When I went to Sweden for my company's 25th anniversary, my colleagues dragged me onto the dance floor and we danced while recording a short video. I shared the photos I took and the video I edited, which helped my colleagues get to know me better. Many of them even sent emails to commemorate the good times we had together. A few days ago when I returned to the company for training, I recorded a video of the happy moments when we celebrated a colleague's birthday, set to the tune of *We Will Rock You*. When I played it for everyone, it unexpectedly became the highlight of the training session. My colleagues said, "From now on, every time we get together, you have to film a segment for us as a keepsake!" Who would have thought that with such a lovely group of colleagues, even someone with a bit of social anxiety like me could be "trained" to become half a social butterfly?

Last month, the vice president of the company's European headquarters left. In her farewell email, she wrote, "You are very nice and kind, and also a very competent person!" These words gave me great encouragement and affirmation. Looking back on the past few years, I feel deeply grateful for the mentors and friends I have met along the way, as I have been lucky enough to find something that I like and am good at. It turns out that being introverted is not a problem, and it's okay to be a "nice person"; seeking authenticity and simplicity is always rewarding. When you use yourself as a guide, you will always find new joy.

About the author

Zimin is currently living in Oxford, UK. She has lived and worked in the UK for 15 years and is now a senior consultant in a pharmaceutical consultancy. She loves life and work, reading, cats, plants and photography.

Days of Commuting to an Island by Boat

Written by: Ji Yang
Translated by: Zhang Bing

Six years ago, in June, I flew from Beijing to London. It was my first time in the UK. When my plane was hovering over London, waiting for clearance to land, I tried to look out the window in search of those well-known landmarks I'd heard so much about, like the London Eye and Big Ben. Unfortunately, I couldn't see anything clearly. However, I did see a river, which I knew was the Thames. It wound its way from the east to the west, splitting London into two. For someone like me visiting this famous city for the first time, anything familiar, even if not completely recognizable, would bring me some comfort and warmth.

I spent my first night in London in a hotel with the postcode SW5. In the UK, a postcode can tell you almost everything about a place, its owners and visitors: the degree of prosperity of the area, the social standing of the owner, the taste of visitors, and much more. The hotel was about a 10-minute-walk away from the London Bridge, justifying the high price of £120 per night. Although it was the cheapest hotel in this area, it was still a significant expense for me. And the room was so small that I had to choose between opening the door and opening my luggage.

I slept soundly and didn't learn until the next morning that there had been a terrorist attack on London Bridge that evening. On June 3rd 2017, terrorists rammed their car into a crowd, wounding and killing many. That day, I took the train from Waterloo station to Southampton, heading towards the Isle of Wight, the southernmost island in the UK. Farewell, London. I had to leave this famous metropolis with fear and confusion before even beginning to savour its beauty and richness.

My story of commuting by boat begins in Southampton, the largest city in Hampshire. It sits on the very southern tip of England and has ferries to the Isle of Wight. Upon arrival, I dropped off my luggage and set off in the direction of the pier. I came across an elderly English gentleman who was probably in his 70s. Since he seemed like a local and in good spirits, I decided to ask him about the pier. We were standing in the middle of a sunken square on Southampton High Street, between West Quay and the old city gate. He pointed to the gate, which was in the opposite direction to the railway station, and told me to go to Town Quay and take the Red Funnel. Due to my limited vocabulary, I failed to grasp the term "Town Quay". I had expected to hear words like "port", "dock", "pier", "jetty", "harbour" or "marina" – anything that has even the slightest connection to boarding a boat. However, I didn't hear any of those. Also, I didn't expect a big city like Southampton to be called just a "town" in English. I later learned that whether a place is called a "town" or "city" depends mainly on whether it accommodates a cathedral. Winchester, for example, despite being smaller than Southampton, has Winchester Cathedral and thus merits being called a city. However, in my understanding back then, a "town" was a rural area larger than a village but smaller than a city, as is true in China. Secondly, the word "quay" and "tourist wharf" were beyond my vocabulary. And besides, what on earth are "Red Chimney" and "Red Funnel"?

Fortunately, I found my way to the pier. I bought a return ferry ticket at Red Funnel's ticket office and boarded the fast ferry to the Isle of Wight. My smooth journey persuaded me that everything was smaller than I had envisioned, yet more convenient than I had imagined.

The Isle of Wight is promoted as an "Area of Outstanding Natural Beauty". It is a diamond-shaped island floating in the southernmost part of England. The northern part faces mainland Britain, while the other end lies across the English Channel from Normandy, France. The 17-mile-long tidal river Medina, flowing from the north to the centre of the Isle of Wight, divides the Cowes into East Cowes and (West) Cowes.

Finally, I settled in Southampton and began my routine of commuting three times a week by either the fast ferry or the large ferry. There are two routes to the Isle of Wight: one is by the fast ferry (Red Jet) to (West) Cowes, and the other was by the large triple-deck ferry – the first deck for cargo and vehicles, the second for passengers, and the third offering scenic views to East Cowes on the eastern bank of the Medina River. The Medina River stretches from the Solent, a strait between the Isle of Wight and mainland Great Britain, all the way to Newport at the heart of the island.

Since I worked in (West) Cowes, I had to cross the Medina River if I took the large ferry.

On the first day of commuting by ferry, the 20-minute journey was quite bumpy. I looked out the window at the moving clouds, full of excitement, but also uncertainty.

In the first few weeks, I took the fast ferry to save time. Most passengers were fellow commuters. Just off the pier is the High Street in (West) Cowes, a pedestrian street paved with black stone that can get particularly slippery on a rainy day. After passing five or six stores along this dark stripe of stone, I turned right when I saw Costa Coffee, a second-hand store and a Marks & Spencer. Following Seaview Road and Moorgreen Road, which wind uphill, I then turned left at No. 54. Initially, the streets and low houses all looked the same to me. The only way for me to avoid getting lost was to drill those street names and house numbers into my head.

It was quite different from my previous work experience. When I was in developing countries, I worked in towering skyscrapers in bustling metropolises like Shanghai and Beijing, followed by a stint in Dubai. Now, in a developed country, I found myself traveling to a remote little industrial park on an isolated island. In the UK, smaller companies and factories are usually nestled in small industrial parks. Next to my office was the warehouse area, opposite a baseball field. Looking around, nothing blocked my view of the sea, which was only a ten-minute walk away.

After fully weighing the pros and cons, I eventually decided to switch to the large ferry. This decision extended my commute from twenty minutes to an hour, but the benefits were also clear: first, unlike the fast ferry which would bounce on waves or get cancelled in high winds, the large ferry was safe and steady. Also, the large ferry was cheaper. With an annual pass, the one-way fare was less than £10. The large ferry also had wi-fi, a bar and a viewing deck, which gave me a holiday vibe on my way to the office. The idea of taking the large ferry was actually inspired by my colleague Matthew. Apart from the longer travel time, the only other inconvenience was that I had to take another boat to cross the Medina River to reach (West) Cowes.

This meant taking the chain boat, the only transport linking the two sides of the river. Although the river is less than 50 metres wide, there is no bridge. And the chain boat, about 15 metres long, ferries a dozen cars and people across the river. Using a chain-drive system, the boat plods across the river, humming and groaning. Each ride costs 50 pence per person or £1.50 per car. Every time I waited for the chain boat, I couldn't help but think, why don't they just build a bridge? A stone arch bridge would save us from all these hurdles! It turned out I wasn't alone in this thought. My Indian colleague Ashley thought the same. He remarked while shaking his head, "Before coming to Britain, I thought Britain was a developed country, but now I am riding on this piece of obsolete junk." He came to the island because his wife started working as a GP here, and he had to find a job as a designer. I guess it's part of life in England to complain a bit about the conservatism and stubbornness of the nation while also enjoying some of its perks. Bringing home fresh eggs from a colleague's free-range chickens isn't something I've been able to do anywhere else in the world.

I remember taking ferries to Gulangyu and Putuoshan, two scenic islands in China where no bridges are built for the sake of local ecosystems. But the chain boat between East and (West) Cowes has existed for decades for other reasons.

One day after work, I was waiting for the chain boat with my colleague Matthew. A sailboat with a high mast passed by, its sail billowing in the wind. The sailors waved to the chain-boat captain and the people on the lookout tower. The queue in front of the pier grew longer and longer. People waited patiently, watching or waving back at the sailors. Suddenly, I understood why there's no bridge. Matthew explained, "A bridge would need to be high enough to let the vessels pass, which means a long ramp that would ruin the old buildings near the banks." It's not simply about building a bridge, but about the conservation of the historical landscape. If a bridge were ever built, it should be a drawbridge like Tower Bridge in London to let ships with high masts sail through.

When given the choice between convenience and tradition, the British almost always choose the latter. They won't sacrifice anything that brings joy or holds value. Over time, I realised that the British prioritise maintaining a balance between progress and traditions over rapid development and efficiency.

In the UK, there's a reluctance to change. Everything simply remains as it is. I've adopted a slower pace of life here, and am no longer stressed about project deadlines or product delivery times. I've also become more patient with commuting. When waiting for the ferry, I leisurely unfold my laptop, and occasionally glance out of the window to see the ferry and chain boat lazily approach, carrying me unhurriedly to the next destination in life.

About the author

Ji Yang is a Master of Science at Zhejiang University and has years of experience as a senior engineer in the energy industry. Yang started to live and work in the UK from 2017. She is fond of art and literature, and is keen on painting and freelance writing.

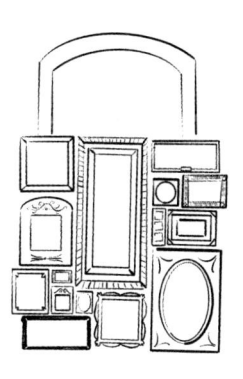

Opening an Art Gallery in London

Written by: Song Guming
Translated by: He Yining

Time flies, and in the blink of an eye, I have been in the UK for fourteen years now. When I arrived in Newcastle for my master's degree in 2009, I never would have imagined that fourteen years later I would still live in the UK, let alone have opened an art gallery in London. From the inception of the idea to engaging with young Chinese artists last summer, and then to finally hosting our first exhibition in September this year, the journey has been bumpy. Yet, here we are, having taken that crucial first step. As 2023 draws to a close, I'd like to share a few insights of things I've learned along the way.

1. The Art World is a Tough Nut to Crack

The art world is like a delicate tapestry, with artists, museums, collectors, galleries, critics, auction houses and other service providers intricately woven together by invisible threads. If you're an outsider, it's hard to get a glimpse of its inner workings. When I decided to open a gallery, I knew almost nothing about the art industry. My only connections to the art world were as a "tourist" in museums and galleries.

Generally, unless you're an artist, there are few paths into the art world. One is to follow in the footsteps of your family (need I say more). Another is to study art history, museology or curating in college, then work in a gallery or auction house, or become an independent curator. A third way is to enter from related fields like finance, logistics or warehousing. The fourth way, which is how I did it, could be called "parachuting".

"Parachuting" means free-falling into the art world from an entirely different background, without any prior experience. It's not impossible, but it's tough. The art world has its unique ecosystem and art is considered a luxury good that doesn't follow typical economic rules. Even if initial investments in a gallery are substantial, cash-flow is often unstable, creating significant barriers to entry.

So why is this world so difficult to break into? It boils down to the industry's opacity, which has long been a point of contention for outsiders. However, in the art world, high prices are intricately linked with affluence, cultivating an atmosphere where discretion, caution and secrecy become the keywords of the industry.

Yet, even being part of the most exclusive circles doesn't guarantee entry into the art world. You need to leverage existing contacts to the max and focus on building a strong network. The art industry in London is quite small, with just a few hundred commercial and non-commercial institutions. In this circle, who you know is of utmost importance. The right people can greatly promote your career. Lacking strong connections can create many difficulties for a newcomer. Over the past two years, I've gone from knowing no one to gradually meeting with mentors, gallery owners, artists and even partners. Among them, one person stands out like a neon sign in my dark art alley.

2. Mr. D

It was a happy coincidence. In October 2021, I attended a short course on art history at the Barbican Centre, which was one of the first in-person classes allowed following the outbreak of the pandemic. That's where I met Mr. D, an American who moved to London. Besides being an avid contemporary art collector, he's a dedicated art critic and author. He had spent decades as a marketing executive at Apple but retired when the pandemic hit. After retiring, he started an independent art review website, updating it punctually and consistently every Monday.

Mr. D is of medium height and has short ginger hair and a neatly trimmed beard. His eyes squint a bit when he gets excited. At first, we were just classmates, though I greatly admired his insight on contemporary artists. The eight-week course flew by, and as it ended, I created a group for our classmates to visit galleries together in the future. Mr. D and I worked together to organise weekend gallery visits and through this, I discovered another side to him.

I realised that his love for art was unparalleled. His website proudly claims to be completely independent, ad-free and sponsor-free, which I found to be entirely true. He'd come up with ten to 20 different exhibitions to put on our weekly schedule, from renowned displays at the National Gallery to obscure shows curated in basements. His meticulous planning left me in awe. He arranged the gallery visits a week in advance based on location, marking them methodically on his calendar. On the day of a visit, nothing short of a hurricane can deter him.

Likewise, his dedication to writing is unrelenting. As a writer, I have great respect for the craft of writing, and even more for the persistence it requires. Since starting his website in early 2022, Mr. D has written daily and weekly without interruption. Once, he had a back injury and was bedridden for three days. On the fourth day, he went out to catch up on the week's exhibitions to ensure his review would be published on Monday.

His writing is straightforward, witty, and offers unique insights. His reviews are concise, combining direct descriptions of the exhibitions with broader reflections on the artists. He follows Jay Rayner's school of criticism and avoids negative reviews of exhibitions he dislikes, emphasising that art appreciation is a highly subjective, personal experience.

About a month ago, Mr. D invited a group of friends and artists, including me, to view over 100 pieces of contemporary art in his private collection. During 20 years of collecting, they were separated into painting, sculpture and installation art and each of them had a story behind it. That Sunday, I lingered among the diverse styles and aesthetics of his collection, marvelling at how Rome wasn't built in a day.

In the two years I've known Mr. D, he has been of immense help to me. He was able to help me decipher industry nuances and resolve issues I encountered while opening my gallery. As a seasoned collector and critic, he helped me steady my parachute and primed me for a soft landing. He is truly an invaluable mentor and friend in my life.

About the author

Song Guming came to the UK to study in 2009 and moved to London in 2011. He works in financial consulting, while his leisure hours are devoted to the Ming Gu Gallery (minggugallery.com), promoting emerging contemporary artists with a focus on traditional East Asian aesthetics. His hobbies include judo, photography and Latin dance.

A Kaleidoscope of Faces

A man shall see faces,
which, if you examine them part by part,
you shall never find good;
but take them together, are not uncomely.

> Francis Bacon
> *Of Beauty*

Helping You Home

Written by: Rebekah Zhao
Translated by: Seth O'Farrell

In December, the weather in the south of England shifts between warmth and cold. What had once been mist and fog had now given way to clear, blue skies.

I hurried out the door, stretching my sore back.

The sun shone brightly on the silent streets, yet there wasn't a single pedestrian in sight. We've lived on this street for over ten years. Normally, at this time of day, passersby would be heading to school, work, the train station or the bus stop. But with the pandemic putting everything under lockdown, the streets were deserted. I used to exchange smiles and greetings with my neighbours as we passed on the pavement. Now, whenever we spotted someone approaching from a distance, we'd quickly cross to the other side of the street, pretending not to notice each other.

Since I no longer work, my days have taken on a peaceful rhythm. I turn off my mobile phone, immerse myself in books, and enjoy the quiet, free from the distractions of conversation. Ever since last year, Kai has been working from home, shouting at his computer daily. I teased him, saying he made as much noise as a flock of pigeons, but I had no way of avoiding him. So, I would roll my eyes and eagerly await those rare moments when the clouds cleared and the fog lifted. "I'm off to get some oxygen!" I'd shout, then dash out the door.

Luckily, while the lockdown policies in the UK shut down towns and cities, the roads and streets remained open. I began spending more time exercising outdoors than I had before.

As I rounded the corner, I came across an elderly English lady. I was about to avoid her when I heard her say, "Can you help me?"

Her expression was earnest. British ladies of her generation often wear heavy makeup when they go out, and I noticed she was wearing not only lipstick but rouge as well. Despite walking with a slight stagger, her face was fresh, her complexion rosy under her thick coat on this chilly day. She wasn't coughing and showed no signs of illness.

"Could you help me carry my shopping bags?" she asked, holding several in her hands.

"Of course, no problem," I said, bending down to take two of the bags from her. She insisted on carrying the other two herself.

She explained that she usually stayed at home but had decided to walk to the nearby Tesco to see what was available and ended up buying more than she'd planned. Halfway back, the bags had become too heavy. In this residential area, there were no taxis to be found.

"I live a few streets away, and I can pay you for the help," she added.

I found her offer charmingly old-fashioned. I wondered if she had family nearby or if she lived alone. It's hard to ask personal questions to a stranger, so instead, I asked her how she had been coping with the pandemic.

"I take good care of myself," she said. "Boris said we should sing *Happy Birthday* three times every time we wash our hands. I sing *God Save the Queen* three times every time I wash my hands."

We both laughed. She went on to say that she has not had a birthday party since her husband's death. But every year she receives a birthday card from her daughter that reads "Happy Birthday".

I asked her if she had ever experienced a pandemic or epidemic before? How did the elderly take precautions in the past?

Oh, she said, there had been one in the 1930s, when she was a teenager living in the countryside. They hung a lot of garlic on the door of their house and sprinkled salt on the ground. Her mother gave the children camomile tea and tonic water.

I said that my hometown sits on the longest river in China and my grandmother would give us chrysanthemum tea, honeysuckle tea and isatis root tea.

She happily listened and asked me what grade I was in.

I was taken aback but also a little delighted. I softly replied that my children have already graduated. That day I wore a bright yellow hooded down jacket and the white hair on the top of my head was hidden under the brim of my hat.

She didn't seem to hear me and continued to talk to herself, unperturbed by anything else, praising me as a good girl.

"You are close to your parents, right?"

I told her that we were close.

"They'll be proud of you for being a good child."

I said they would. She went on to say:

"Children are very well-behaved when they're of school age, just like little angels."

Then she suddenly fell silent and stopped talking.

I realised her memory was a little hazy. She might feel embarrassed if she knew that the person carrying her bags was not a schoolgirl.

We walked forward slowly and in silence. When she arrived at a small roundabout, she looked back and forth for a while before moving forward. The bags in my hand became heavy.

After crossing a large street and turning into a street of terraced houses, she suddenly said, "We're here." She stopped in her tracks. I couldn't tell which door was her house, so I asked:

"Would you like me to take the bags in the door for you?"

"No, thank you, I can take them in myself," she said, without expression.

I stopped insisting. Watching her turn around and look for something on her clothes, I patiently waited, thinking that she might have something else to say.

Instead, she took out her wallet, handed me a £10 note and said:

"This is for you."

Without even thinking, I reached out my hand and took the note. Ever since the pandemic, we had all been paying electronically and had not touched banknotes for two years. Touching it with my hand, my fingertips made a slight rustling noise, both familiar and real.

When I attended my daughter's school Christmas concert in the UK, several students with cherry lips and pearly white teeth stood at the entrance door to greet the guests. A boy came up to me and asked, "Can I take your coat for you, madam?" I took off my coat and gave it to him. Following the instructions whispered to me by an English friend standing behind me, I gave the boy a coin. He happily thanked me and hung my coat in the cloakroom for me.

I put the note into my pocket, only to take it out and hand it back to her, saying:

"Thank you for the tip. I was going to the gym today but walking with you, I feel that I've saved myself the journey as I've done more exercise than I would have done on the stepper."

She collected the money, put it in her wallet, and said pensively:

"Catherine didn't think I would be able to go shopping. Now she'll be surprised to see how much I've bought."

"Next time you go shopping, call me in advance and I will drive to pick you up," I said, taking out my phone.

She didn't reply but continued, "Catherine comes to delliver items to me every Tuesday. This week she was on holiday, not working. She called to say she would not come until next Tuesday."

I wasn't sure if Catherine was a social worker or a friend. I waved and said goodbye. I told her my street and house number twice before leaving, adding that if she wanted to go shopping by herself next time, she could knock on the door and call me any time. She nodded and looked at me with a dull look in her eyes but a clear smile on her face.

Soon enough, lockdown was lifted. People passed by my door as usual, but I never saw her again.

As I crossed that corner, I would occasionally think of the strange old woman who made me feel like a secondary school student.

About the author

Rebekah Zhao moved to the UK in 1994. She is a PhD in Chinese History. She taught at university and secondary school, and was a freelance writer. She has published *The Reading Experience at UK Primary Schools* and *The Interaction of Eastern and Western Art*.

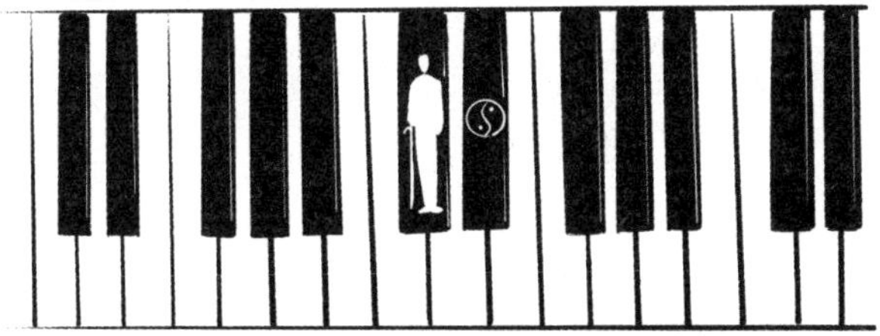

A Musical Encounter

Written by: Xiao Chunduan
Translated by: Sun Shulang

As a child, reading *Pipilu and Luxixi**, I fervently wished to own a "little doctor". With such a tiny, all-knowing companion, I wouldn't need to worry about failing exams due to my laziness. Instead, on the exam, I could simply pop the "little doctor" in my ear who would answer all the questions for me with great ease. I would then achieve outstanding grades and win the admiration of my teachers and parents – Haha! And so, I scoured for expired canned goods, always reluctant to open those that were still within their shelf lives. Such wishful thinking has been going on for years, during which I've taken many exams. I've never found a little doctor to help me on the exams, but the memory of my childhood innocence warms my heart. Time dulls my fantasies and diminishes the surprises in my life as my days in England stretch on in monotony. While I hesitate to boast about my modest academic progress, I have gained valuable insights into culture and life. The most thrilling experience was my encounter in the piano room, and before I fully wake from that dream, I'd love to share it with you.

My university boasts a renowned art centre; the largest in the UK outside of London. It houses two large concert halls, two theatres, a cinema and a music centre. Approximately 250,000 people visit it annually, and world-class orchestras and renowned artists frequently perform there. Chances are that you will brush shoulders with a world-famous maestro while visiting. Compared to performances back in China, the tickets to concerts here are really a great deal. To promote music to the public, the music centre often hosted free concerts, usually held at noon, and known as "musical lunches". Given my tight budget, I became a regular at these events.

The other thing that drew me to the music centre was the pianos. There was one performance hall and nine piano rooms, seven of which were accessible to students and staff. The piano rooms at my undergraduate school back home always drew me in, despite their high fees and shabby interiors. I was willing to spend money to play there, often making the long trip back and forth from my dormitory. Now that I'm in the UK, surrounded by well-equipped piano rooms I can access anytime, I can't let this opportunity go to waste. Playing the piano became my solace amid the burdens of tuition and living expenses in this capitalist society.

The pianos were spread over two floors, with the stone rooms downstairs being the best. The temperature in the stone rooms was lower than it was elsewhere, and as soon as you stepped inside, you were enveloped by a refreshing chill. Touching the stone walls felt like touching ice. Whenever I was anxious, I would rush into these stone rooms, which would calm down my mind at once. Even with double doors, one could still hear the sounds from other rooms. The music centre was a hub of talent. Huddled in a stone room, I could always hear the exquisite sound of a coloratura soprano or a magnificent piano cadenza from the other side of the wall. At such moments, the beginner's pieces I was playing suddenly paled in comparison, and I often found myself holding my breath, listening intently, and totally getting lost in the music. Once, while I was playing *Für Elise*, the saxophone player from the next room started to accompany me from the next room. Oh, how tender and charming *Für Elise* sounds on a saxophone! I couldn't help but slow down to play to his rhythm. Hearing the fine sound and brilliant rhythm of the saxophone, I was so captivated that I started to wonder about the person on the other side of the wall...He must be a young gentleman, handsome and elegant. Alas! Had I not been so shy (this is certainly a product of my Chinese culture), I would have popped in to see his face. But perhaps this was for the best, leaving a beautiful image in my mind.

The pianos at the music centre were quite good, but they were not the best. The best piano on campus was in the church next to the music centre. It was a baby grand piano, not only stunning in appearance but also flawless in tone. When all the lights in the hall were on, sitting in front of that piano made you feel so elegant, as if you were at your own personal recital. Every time I passed by and found the hall unoccupied, I would excitedly run in to play the piano, feeling nothing but gratitude for this heavenly gift. However, I didn't expect that one day my "little doctor" would appear out of nowhere.

That day, I pulled back the long curtains to reveal a blue sky and budding trees, prompting me to turn off my computer and step outside for a walk. Bathed in warm sunlight and inhaling fresh air, I felt rejuvenated, as if I had just completed a forty-nine-day retreat. Embracing nature, my feet instinctively took me toward the art centre. As I passed the church and found it empty, a sense of secret delight washed over me.

The piano was positioned in the northeast corner of the hall, separated from the outside lawn by floor-to-ceiling windows. The lush green grass beyond was so inviting that my fingers instinctively began to play "The Happy Farmer". I was never a diligent student; for instance, when my teacher insisted on warming up with scales, I ignored the advice and followed my own inclinations. While my classmates started with pieces like John Thompson's "Hanon Studies", I couldn't wait to dive into Richard Clayderman's works as soon as I learned to read music, practising diligently on my own. After a few lessons, I found the pace of my teacher's instruction too slow, so I decided to teach myself. As a result, my piano technique remained weak and I found it difficult to elevate myself to the next level.

However, I did enjoy some compositions, such as Bach's "Minuet in G Major" and Schubert's "Moment Musical in F Minor". They never grew old and always remained fresh. Each time I played them, I came across some new challenges. For example, their final notes need just the right touch: too soft, and the ending seemed abrupt; too loud, and it felt exaggerated. A tiny variation in legato, staccato, speed and dynamics could make a huge difference in the performance. Pondering over these nuances, I finished the "Minuet in G Major", which aroused a few crisp claps from the silence. I looked around and saw a pair of hands and a head sticking out from behind a screen. "Very good!" the person said.

I smiled back and continued practising. Having been in England for half a year, I had grown accustomed to the friendly compliments of the locals.

The British might be one of the friendliest nations in the world, often giving higher praise than deserved. "Very good" could only be equated to something like "not bad" or "alright" in Chinese.

Realising the importance of improving step-by-step, I started practising scales on the keyboard. Speed! Dynamics! As these thoughts swirled in my mind, I climbed the scales faster and faster, hitting the keys with increasing intensity. Suddenly, I noticed a shadow approaching. Looking up, I saw a well-dressed elderly man, strong and healthy, though on crutches. His serious expression made me a bit uneasy, so I asked timidly, "Would you like to use the piano?"

The old man came to me and said, "Do you segment your scales while you play them?" Though his tone was not quite warm, his eyes were sparkled with kindness.

"Um? Hmm... I'm not sure, I've never thought of it."

"Watch this..." The old man transferred the right crutch to his left hand, freeing his right hand to play a scale on the keyboard with great rhythm, then played it again in my hurried way, "Have you noticed the difference?"

I gave a silly grin.

"Which one sounds better?"

"The first one, it has more character," I replied. The old man could not stand the fact that I played the beautiful piece in that terrible way, so he rushed over to stop me.

"Well, you played Bach quite well earlier, and you have a good sense of music. But focusing only on speed and dynamics in scales will make the practice dull, and that is not what music is meant to be."

The old man then opened the piano lid and began explaining the articulation principles of piano to me, using many unfamiliar physics terms. However, I grasped the gist: to use softness to counter hardness, much like the brilliance of Tai Chi's "using four ounces to deflect a thousand pounds", effortlessly redirecting one's opponent's powerful attack with a gentle push.

Figuring the old man must be a master, I asked him to play a piece. He happily agreed, throwing his crutches aside and removing his wrist supports before sitting down to play. His hands moved swiftly across the keys, covering an expansive range with breathtaking speed, creating a majestic and intricate tapestry of sound. I was totally stunned by his powerful performance. When he finished, I was so awestruck that I forgot to applaud. Only after regaining my senses did the word "top-notch" come to my mind.

The old man asked, "Would you like to learn piano from me?"

Wow...I was speechless.

Later, I learned that the piece he played that day was a Chopin rhapsody. The old man had graduated from the University of Oxford and his children earned their degrees at the Royal Academy of Music. They are all accomplished musicians and perform concerts from time to time.

There is more to the story, but I've decided to end it here, on this happy note. Pun intended.

Pipilu and Luxixi is a beloved Chinese children's literature series by the renowned author Zheng Yuanjie, following the imaginative adventures of the siblings Pipilu and Luxixi as they explore fantastical worlds and learn valuable life lessons.

About the author

Dr. Xiao Chunduan is a literature PhD and is a professor at Jinan University's College of Foreign Languages. She supervises doctoral students in overseas Chinese literature and conducts research at the Overseas Chinese Literature and Chinese Media Research Center. Recognised as a distinguished young scholar and part of the "Double Hundred Talents" at Jinan University, she has also been a visiting scholar at the University of Cambridge.

Dr. Xiao holds several professional roles, including:

Director of the British Literature Division of the Chinese Association for the Study of Foreign Literature;

Member of the World Ethnic Literature Professional Committee of the Comparative Language and Culture Association;

Director of the Guangzhou Association of Overseas Returnees from Europe and America;

Additionally, she has worked as a translator for London ECI and has translated programmes for television networks like the BBC.

My Welsh Friend Lloyd

Written by: Sun Lin
Translated by: Li Shu

I first met Lloyd in 1988 in Portsmouth, an island city in southern England. Thirty-five years passed in the blink of an eye.

At that time, we were under the same supervisor and funded by the same company to do research projects, the results of which were written into our dissertation. We lived in Southsea, worked in Havant, and went to the University of Portsmouth now and then to have a meeting with our supervisor or attend classes. I remember on my first day at work, Lloyd invited me to have a drink in the evening. From then on, we often went out for drinks, sometimes with our new friends. I became familiar with the names of some drinks I typically ordered, even though the bartender would occasionally serve the wrong one due to my mispronunciation. I had been a non-drinker, but after frequenting pubs, I got accustomed to the noise. My friends and I always went to a couple of pubs in one night where drinks were paid in turn, and I was able to finish a pint of beer in each of the pubs. Pub hopping at night made it easy to see the other side of British people: gentlemen would behave like hooligans, peeing on streets and whistling at girls passing by.

We commuted by regional rail for work and classes when we first arrived in Portsmouth. Later we bought cars and often hung out on weekends. What I remember most vividly were the warships in Portsmouth, cycling on the Isle of Wight, Brighton Beach, airshows, open-air music festivals and various museums. If a museum had a steam locomotive, we would spend most of the day trying to figure out how it worked.

Lloyd's Chinese name was given by my father. "Lloyd", according to him, means "grey hair" in Welsh. Neither of us had girlfriends when we first met, so we would invite girls to go out with us at every opportunity. A Japanese girl and her friend lived near us, and they would occasionally join us. One time, she asked why the staff ignored her when she would like to order another drink or dessert at a restaurant. Our British friend asked her to repeat their conversation. She said the staff member said, "Would you like to have some dessert?", and she answered, "Yes, thank you." My friend said it was probably because of her soft voice that the staff only heard "Thank you" which usually went together with "No". Since then, she started to say "Yes, please" instead, and the staff waited for her to order as expected.

A year later, we were both unhappy with our flatmates and decided to share a flat. As Lloyd spoke with a heavy accent, the estate agent once joked with us, "I can't understand either one of you. How do you two understand each other?" But we did! And we talked about everything under the sun. I still remember our discussions on idioms with similar meanings in Chinese and English, such as "teach grandma to suck eggs" and "ashtray on a motorbike".

Our parents soon got to know each other. I spent Christmas that year with Lloyd at his parents' home in southwest Wales, one of the warmest times of my life in the UK. His mother took great care of me, making me feel the warmth of family in a foreign country. At that time, we walked their dog together and visited the church where Lloyd sang in the choir as a child, though he never went to church in Portsmouth. In the afternoons, we accompanied his father to the pub, and his mother told me with a smile that it was her husband's happiest moment. According to Lloyd, he was taken by his father to taste beer when he was still in primary school. Despite the distance, the life here had much in common with that in the countryside and small town where I grew up. Regulars of the pub had known each other for decades, some of whom had never left Wales. Many of Lloyd's friends stayed where they grew up and now had children of their own. In the pub, people would occasionally come up to me, telling me that it was their first time greeting an Asian. A few years later, Lloyd got a job abroad. I made a special trip to visit his parents when I came to the UK. I noticed that the kitten embroidered with Xiang Embroidery (or Hunan Embroidery, one of the traditional folk arts of China) that I had given them during my first visit still hung prominently in their living room. I accompanied his father to the pub again, where people were eagerly discussing the new South Korean factory in Wales, but were confused about Chinese, South Korean, Japanese and other Asian brands.

On another occasion, Lloyd invited my parents to live in his room when they travelled to the UK in 1990, while he stayed with his friend for a month. Three decades on, after leaving the UK, I worked and lived in various cities and countries, keeping in touch with Lloyd. When I heard the news of his mother's passing, I was brought to tears.

I moved to Singapore in 1991, while Lloyd found a job in Germany. Two years later, we reunited in Heidelberg and went to a pub to discuss the cocktails Leibniz might have drunk. In 1993, we both worked in Heidelberg. In the mid-90s when Lloyd returned to the UK to look for a job, I sent him a job advertisement from a Singaporean research institute that recruited employees in Europe, and he got the job on his first try. In the following years, our families travelled together in Singapore, Malaysia and the Philippines. Lloyd and his wife took the opportunity to visit India, Indonesia, China, Thailand and Cambodia, among other countries. Once, they joined a tour group to Malaysia, and it just so happened that my younger brother was planning to travel there as well, so they travelled together. Lloyd later joined a multinational software company and was sent to France. Unfortunately, my child was too young at the time for us to all explore the "Route des Vins" together.

We always sent each other our best wishes at Christmas, during Spring Festival, and every year on our birthdays, even if we worked and lived in different cities. In 2010, after my children started school, my family travelled to the UK and went to Wales to visit Lloyd and his wife. Our friendship has endured many years, many changes and many turns. I feel lucky to have Lloyd as a friend for life.

About the author

Sun Lin, a native of Hunan province, has worked in various institutions, including research institutes, multinational companies, startups, government and universities. He enjoys travelling and writing in his spare time.

My Distant Neighbour Bernice

Written by: Xiaohei
Translated by: Amy Culver

In the first decade of living in the UK, I made two major accomplishments: I earned a Master's Degree in Science from a middling UK university and bought a two-storey house with front and back gardens in Zone 3 in North London during the economic downturn. The neighbourhood was pleasant and there were cherry blossoms lining the street, filling it with the beautiful colours of spring.

I met Tony on the day I moved in. He was the British neighbour to my right. "Hello, you alright? The weather is…" And with that, the acquaintance was made. On the fourth day, I met Raj, the Indian neighbour to my left. We had a three-minute chat and became friends.

As a writer, and therefore a homebody, I barely spoke to other neighbours in the few years that followed. Then one day, a middle-aged white woman with pronounced cheekbones and a pointy chin walked over to me from across the street, looking upset.

At the time, I was removing a large hedge by the street with the help of a handyman. The hedge was growing quickly and it took too much work to maintain it. The woman stood very close to me, and remarked coldly, "What you're doing is wrong."

I was taken aback and completely speechless. She carried on, "Birds have nests in these hedges. You can't dig them up."

I pretended I didn't hear her and said nothing at the time, but I was fuming inside. "This woman is a bit nosy!" I thought. She walked off after not getting a response out of me.

A few days later, I happened to bump into her again in the street. I thought she would be annoyed with me for what happened and would just ignore me. Instead, she started making small talk, "How was your weekend?"

I hurriedly put on a polite smile and said, "I visited Chatsworth House. Oh, it is grand like a palace, the garden alone is over a hundred acres…"

She broke in and said in a more serious tone, "For only one family to live in such a big house, don't you think it's unfair?"

I didn't know what to say, and thought perhaps she was a hypocritical leftie. But she looked sincere.

I stood around while she went on about how the estate should belong to the people. Then, all of a sudden her voice softened up and got more enthusiastic, "I must invite you over for a cup of tea."

About a year later, I found a handwritten invitation to tea in my letterbox. I only learned then that her name was Bernice (meaning "bringer of victory"). I checked out her house number, it was about 150 steps from my house, making us "distant neighbours".

I accepted her invitation. After a few cups of tea, we were still deeply engaged in conversation. I learned that Bernice worked in a university library in London. Her husband, Oliver, was a poet. Aside from a few *ad-hoc* jobs here and there, he spent most of his time sitting at home, like me, gazing out of the window.

Bernice liked talking about current affairs and politics. Her father was a secondary school teacher. She told me that from her great grandfather on to her, her family had always voted Labour in every general election. She would also worry about issues that were tens of thousands of miles away. She had a pact with her friends to buy only second-hand clothes from charity shops, in order to help famine victims in Africa. She also boycotted discount stores, as the cheap products they sold were made by child labourers in poor countries. I was touched by the sensibilities and sense of justice she demonstrated throughout our conversation. She said, "We need to do the right thing," which stuck with me.

As I was leaving, I extended a formal invitation to Bernice and Oliver to come to my place for dinner at a time that suited them.

I would have never guessed that my budding relationship with Bernice would be curtailed after that meal.

I opted to cook, wanting them to try the Western food I make at home. I made steaks, which are a personal favourite, and therefore something I make well. They arrived as I was busy in the kitchen.

When Bernice came in with a glass of red wine, I was focused on flipping the steaks. I noticed how she looked cold as I turned around. "Oh, I am so sorry. I didn't mention that I was a vegan," she said while looking uncomfortable. I told her not to worry as I could make her the Chinese staple of stir-fried tomatoes and eggs.

I served the steaks and suddenly had a feeling that Bernice was glaring at me. "Did you see the latest news?" she said in a concerned tone. "Global warming is intensifying, and it's threatening our existence!"

As I returned the pan to the stove, I responded casually, "Is it that bad?"

Bernice pointed at the steaks, "Cows are some of the main contributors. According to statistics published by scientists, "a cow's fart is more damaging to the atmosphere than the farts of a hundred people put together."

I involuntarily tilted my head to one side and burst out laughing. Bernice was annoyed, she exclaimed, "I wasn't joking!"

I quickly shut up. She then said, "You should become a vegan too."

I thought she was joking, but she looked serious. I started feeling uneasy.

I pretended to agree in hopes of preserving a convivial mood over dinner, "Yeah, sure!"

"Do you mean it?"

"Of course."

She cheered, and cracked a smile.

For the rest of the meal, fast-talker Bernice continued emphasising the importance of being vegan, trying to make us realise that we could all become world-saving heroes if we gave up steak.

I made the decision that night to sever ties with Bernice. The reasons were simple: I wouldn't give up steak and I didn't want her to think of me as a promise-breaker.

It was just that I was never left in peace again. Whenever I had steak again, I could hear Bernice's words of warning echoing in my head: a cow's fart is more damaging to the atmosphere than the farts of a hundred people put together.

When I walked around different British towns and saw various charity shops, or when I saw news about environmentalists protesting...I couldn't help but feel that my distant neighbour Bernice was somehow already everywhere, her presence manifesting in layered vignettes that seemed to follow me incessantly, never leaving me alone.

About the author

Xiaohei, a native to Chengdu, Sichuan Province, is a Chinese writer living in the UK. To date, he has published over a million words across diverse genres. He is also a noted translator, known for his translation of *Wild Swans: Three Daughters of China*. His first novel *Gently, I Leave* (published by Writers Publishing House) was critically acclaimed by *China Reading Weekly* as a breakthrough in new immigrants' novels.

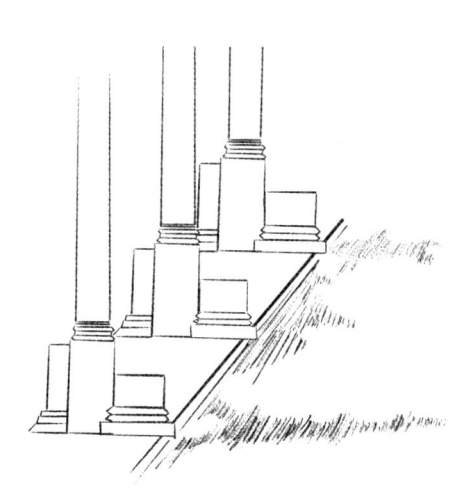

Strangers

Written by: Zhang Yidong
Translated by: Guo Xiyue

Aside from enjoying new scenery, the best part about travelling is chatting with strangers. I love jotting down our conversations, as it makes for entertaining reading once I'm back home. Below, I'd like to treat you, dear reader, to three memorable conversations I've had with strangers.

The first transpired on Saturday, 12th March, 2021 in the city of Bath. The streets were teeming with people, more tourists than locals, it seemed. The Romans built a massive thermal bath here in 60 AD. That's right, a bath! It was a great way to make use of the natural hot springs bubbling up from a low-lying area. The surrounding hills were conveniently packed with cream-coloured stone, perfect for building. It's as if Mother Nature had handed the city a spa kit!

As time went on, the area evolved into a city, and what better name for it than "Bath"? The old town is well preserved, with a unique local feeling about all of the buildings, both old and new. Between its picturesque hills, thermal waters and sunshine, this charming little city attracts millions of tourists every year.

Coffee in hand, I headed down to the River Avon. A friendly-looking woman smiled at me, and I smiled back. She asked me in English if I could take a photo of her. Of course, I was happy to oblige. As I returned her phone, I casually asked her in Chinese if she was from China. She replied, "Sorry, what did you say?" Flustered, I quickly responded, "Sorry, you don't speak Chinese?" She laughed and responded in perfect Chinese, "You speak Chinese! Let's chat in Chinese."

We chatted for about a minute on the side of the road. She was from Shanghai and had been living in the UK for five years. She studied in London and after getting her master's degree, found a job in the UK. Now she lives in Oxford. She told me she's quitting her job in March to return to Shanghai. Her reason? First, although the company is very good, her boss, who is Romanian, has been making her life difficult. Apparently, due to Romania's historical ties to socialism, he holds a strong bias against her and always gives her the toughest tasks. Secondly, she snagged a ticket back to Shanghai last winter for RMB 28,000, and if she doesn't go, that expensive ticket will go to waste. That sounded like a solid reason to me. During the COVID era, a ticket to China could cost as much as RMB 90,000, excluding the cost of mandatory isolation upon entry. RMB 28,000 was quite a bargain.

The second person I want to highlight is a young man who worked for the United Nations. He was from Yunnan Province in China, but spoke Mandarin like a Northerner. He also looked like a northern Chinese boy; strong and athletic. I spent a few minutes listening to his story, and boy, he did have a tale to tell!

I met him at a coffee house not far from a small train station where everyone was seeking refuge from the rain. He bought a cup of hot tea and sat down next to me. The first thing he said was that he works for the United Nations. A few young Chinese people in the room were surprised and expected him to tell us more about his daily work at the UN.

He had earned two master's degrees in London, and during his studies, he interned at the UN. The head of his department noticed his talent and made him a consultant, eventually signing him on as a full-time employee at the UN. It was a rare opportunity. The UN is known for being a slow-moving organization and it is difficult to get new people into the system.

According to him, graduates applying for positions at the UN have to take the UN Civil Service Examination. This exam takes a year to complete, and even if you pass and get an internship, the chances of being promoted into a full-time position are slim to none. The bureaucrats who work for the UN lead a cushy life.

He was disappointed to learn that his boss, an economist with a few university professorships, did not know how to use Excel. He would never forget the day when he performed some statistical calculations in Excel in front of a group of senior UN employees who watched in awe and praised him a genius.

Last year, he was summoned to UN Headquarters in New York. Before his plane even landed, he was scammed out of $3,000 by a fake New York landlord syndicate. They had stolen a landlord's identity information and posted a rental ad online. During a few email exchanges, they convinced him to wire the first month's rent and deposit. After the money was sent, they demanded another three months' rent upfront. That's when he realised he'd been scammed.

After he landed, he reported the incident to the police, who informed him that the bank account receiving the funds was based in Las Vegas and out of their jurisdiction. They shrugged it off. On his first night in New York, he ended up sleeping on a mattress he found on the street. His British bank had detected fraud and frozen his card, leaving him unable to check into a hotel.

And thus, New York welcomed this young UN officer with open arms.

He spent three months living in New York City. This curious young man decided to explore the neighbourhood of Brooklyn. Within five minutes, he found himself surrounded and robbed by several men. He made a risky move and didn't back down, instead he raised his hands in resistance. After receiving a few punches and kicks, he managed to escape. After he returned home, his Chinese roommate shared some local wisdom: New Yorkers carry two wallets. One only contains a few dollars, and is the one they're willing to sacrifice to muggers.

He said the New York subway was unimaginably dirty and smelled of urine. He witnessed drunks kicking passengers off the platform. Outside his rented place, drug addicts would gather at dawn to inject themselves right on the kerb. He also spent time in Chicago, where a local friend introduced him to a website showing the coordinates of daily shootings and violence. He showed us a screenshot from his mobile phone, revealing at least 20 shootings in Chicago that day, densely marked on the map.

After three months in the US, he was thrilled to be back in London. He left his hard-earned job at the UN for a new job in London, beginning the following autumn. He had planned to travel home for Chinese New Year and had spent over RMB 30,000 on flights, but those plans were scuppered by the pandemic.

He is passionate about outdoor sports and plans to climb the Alps next month. He showed me a video taken in Wales, where the mountaintops are windy and snowy, and the peaks are as sharp as knife blades, making them quite a challenging climb.

He was born in Kunming, Yunnan Province. His father is called Pumi, and his mother is called Dai. His father was the first one from his hometown to attend Peking University, and he is a few years older than me. He led a student activity, and when I mentioned a certain name, he immediately recognised it as one of his father's good friends. What an extraordinary coincidence that this young man I randomly met in a crowd could have a connection to me through his father.

His father and I had a mutual friend. I am very glad that his father's graduation was not affected by that activity, and he was still assigned a very good job in the non-ferrous metal industry and settled down in Kunming. After China's economic reforms and opening, he ventured into the market and found great success as an entrepreneur. Sadly, his father's later years were marred by alcohol poisoning and bipolar disorder.

The young man's mother probably attended a good university, though we didn't get a chance to go into her story. He did mention that his mother was an alumnus of an ethnic secondary school in Beijing and knew the school management team well. When he studied at Beijing Nationalities High School, his mother told him about the many shady practices in the school. This young man was so upright and honest that he reported these stories to the media, causing shockwaves at the Beijing Municipal Education Bureau.

He was telling me about a misadventure in Barcelona that cost him his Canon DSLR camera, as the rain began to let up and the cafe started to empty. I reluctantly bid farewell to this courageous, intelligent and worldly young man.

Roger, the third person I met, is a typical elderly Londoner. His face is a charming blend of rosy cheeks and pale white skin punctuated by a kindly nose that seems almost half the length of a baseball cap. His perfect diction and even tone make him sound like the BBC. I stumbled upon Roger while he was fishing along the riverbank. He had just arrived and was sorting out his fishing gear. I stopped by to say hello. He was enthusiastic and answered all my questions which quickly led me to abandon my walk and begin a lively conversation with him.

His fishing spot is a marina connected to the Thames by two small aqueducts. Many boats were moored in the rectangular water, serving as homes for some of their owners. In the past, I watched a film and thought that living on a boat in London sounded romantic. However, seeing these houses floating on the water in person didn't quite evoke envy. It seemed more like a budget-friendly way of life. It is very cold on the boat in winter, and there is no sewerage pipe on the boat, so residents use a chemical toilet that requires them to dispose of their own waste. The boats depend on water and electricity hookups, making it impossible to take them very far from land.

Roger's fishing was unlike anything I had ever seen. He hung a worm on a hook, and then placed a small porous plastic bottle filled with a handful of live rice worms about 30cm away. He'd cast the line, let it sink, and then tighten it. Without using a float, he determined whether or not there was a fish by observing the shaking of the rod. He fished for cold-water fish and caught a very large salmon last week. We talked about everything from fishing to housing. Roger recalled how in the 1960s, most of the houses in London were built by the government, and citizens paid rent to the government. Dissatisfaction led to reforms and several strikes, and then transformed public housing into commercial properties. All of this played a part in making London one of the world's most expensive cities.

Roger started his own business when he was young, publishing a local magazine that was delivered free to restaurants, cafes and other commercial outlets in the community. It ran on adverts for income. He did well enough to enjoy a comfortable retirement. His youngest son had just gotten married. Traditional Brits like Roger spend lavishly on weddings and even more on funerals. My last landlord Lizz's friend had to wait a month for her husband's funeral due to the extensive preparations and costs involved.

Amusingly, after discussing funerals with Roger, one of my phone apps pushed an ad suggesting I start making a financial plan for my own funeral. Roger was a chatterbox, and we discussed the Russia-Ukraine war, refugees, petrol price hikes, driving in London and the travails of parking. I was pleasantly surprised that my English was good enough to converse on such a variety of topics.

Roger paused for a moment to check his line and when he saw the bait was still there, he shook his head and cast it back into the water. I took that as my cue to leave, and wished him good luck in catching another salmon.

About the author

Zhang Yidong, moved to the UK from Beijing in 2021. He is now a FinTech practitioner in London. In his spare time, he enjoys writing and recording interesting life insights.

Like Planes in the Night –
a Driving Classical Music *Aficionado* and a
Photographer Wearing the Paperboy's Cap

Written by: Chen Yan
Translated by: Neil McCallum

The car's peculiar driver listens to classical music

Once, when on a business trip to London, I arrived at Heathrow airport in the early hours of the morning. Having passed through customs and grabbed my suitcase after it had gone round and round the conveyor belt, I finally got to the exit. There really isn't much difference between day and night at an international airport. At the exit, there was a crowd of people, and it took a few tries to find my taxi driver. The driver had been waiting around for a long time, and hadn't picked up my calls. I expected the driver to greet me, as most English people do, but he didn't at first. After a day of rushing about, customs and baggage claim being useless when I got there, my patience was wearing thin. Although we both briefly said "hello" and "thanks", there was a clear sense of impatience in the air.

    I was in a hurry to go home, and he was in a hurry to take me to my destination. We both strode quickly towards the car park. We didn't waste any words; we just wanted to escape the airport as soon as possible. I got into the car, and he calmly sat down in the front after having put my suitcase in the boot. He started the engine, and I immediately heard classical music emanating from the speakers. In that very moment, my impatience and exhaustion washed away. It was as if all the din from the airport five minutes earlier was stuck outside the window.

    A tall, broad, bullish taxi driver with a bad temper can also listen to classical music. The music started when the engine started, and something about the driver indicated to me that he listened to it often – he wasn't just trying to show off. He knew the roads well and overtook others gracefully. His skill as a driver and his refined taste in music made me see him in a new light. My mum and dad always had friends from the world of classical music who'd say to me: just because someone listens to classical music doesn't make them a refined person. Historically, autocrats and evil people have either enjoyed or played classical music. But I think that anyone who listens to classical music can't be all bad. Deep down in their heart, there must be some uncorrupted areas that are enlivened when enjoying music.

I decided to strike up a conversation with the driver about classical music, but I was so tired that I slept all the way home. The car pulled in to stop, and the driver called out to me a few times before I woke up. "Sorry, I fell asleep and didn't hear you speaking." He said, "No worries. It really is late now." Then we parted ways with the same thank you routine; the mood and atmosphere were very different from when we first met. Perhaps it was the impact of time or the power of music, but our moods were calmer. I spent about an hour with this driver. I don't even know his name or where he lived, but together, in silence, we listened to several pieces of classical music on the road from one side of London to the other, from west to east.

John the photographer

John is a middle-aged photographer hired to photograph various events related to his employer. In this era of self-media where anyone can write, direct, act and publish their own works with a mobile phone, he always carries a heavy SLR camera and telephoto and short focal length lenses. His appearance is very recognisable, not because of his figure, but because of his clothes. He likes to wear long, waterproof and windproof coats, and his shoes are usually indigo or dark brown suede. If the occasion is more formal, he will wear a shirt and a tie or bow tie. However, no matter the season, regardless of whether he is indoors or outdoors, he always wears a plaid paperboy cap, which is quite stylish. As a person who cares about appearances, I am inclined to pay more attention to men who dress well. Living in the UK, where people pay attention to the "dress code", it is a pleasure to observe what men and women of all ages wear on different occasions and in different seasons.

However, John seemed to have sort of dislike for me. Over the course of a few years, we'd cross paths a few times a year because of my work in the media. When waiting to conduct an interview, there was always some downtime before the interviewee arrived, during which it seemed appropriate to make polite conversation. It was during these moments that I sensed he held something against reporters like me, who both wrote and took pictures. It's as if he felt that we were somehow inadequate and stealing his job.

When I met him again a few years ago at the annual Spring Festival celebration at Trafalgar Square in central London, he was different from his usual self. This annual celebration is not only a major event for the Chinese community, but also a major event for London. Visiting this celebration every year means entering a battle of wits with tall local media photographers and on-site security guards. These photographers' images are either taken to compete for timeliness or to make money. They demonstrate a kind of wolfish nature rarely witnessed in the British workplace. These photographers are seasoned at warding off journalists like me with their long lenses. But not John. His photos are released exclusively so he doesn't need to compete for the first release.

I arrived at the celebration early, hoping to snag a spot that would allow me the best angles. It hadn't crossed my mind that John would also be there. As usual, we said hello to one another. John knew that I was doing double duty as a photographer and reporter, and on this occasion he very kindly allowed me to have a spot in front of him. While waiting for the show to start, he helped me defend my "territory" several times. He also taught me how to capture the coveted shot of the lion flying over the dome of the National Gallery during the lion dance. This was the first time I had ever gotten that shot in my entire career. The next day, this photo went on the front page of the publication I was working for. When my manager praised me, I silently said in my heart thanks to John.

I was humbled by his proactive offer of help that day. Perhaps he thought that since he couldn't get rid of me, he should just get along with me. But I believe his intention was simply to be kind. His thoughtfulness warmed my heart.

I still remember that before the event started, the guests were socialising in the VIP tent with their hot drinks, chatting and shivering in the cold wind. Talking about transformations in the industry, John, who has been shooting this event for over a decade, said with emotion, "Another year, and I am a year older." I always thought he considered himself to be above us, but it was touching to see him be vulnerable. That humanised him considerably in my mind.

During our hectic lives, there will always be many people and things who pass us by. Although these encounters may amount to nothing and the journey itself is not necessarily thrilling, the fragments of these warm memories will sometimes come to mind. This is the spice of life. With them, a clear noodle soup can be transformed into a broth of a hundred flavors. And, it is because of these ephemeral meetings that I feel more alive.

About the author

Chen Yan has lived in London for over a decade. As a former correspondent, she has written for publications such as *Sing Tao Daily*, *Southern Daily* and *Photography Travel Magazine*. Later, she worked for many marketing and communications companies, playing a small role in Sino-British commercial and cultural exchanges. In her spare time, she likes to resume her identity as a writer, using words to record bits and pieces of British life and beautiful things such as music and art.

Could True Love Be Like This?

Written by: Sun Hong
Translated by: Gan Lin

Sometimes romance isn't found in movies and books but in everyday life and fleeting moments. Recently, I visited Leigh-on-Sea, a small seaside town in the east of England. Those two days were blessed with rare, bright sunny weather that drew out both locals and visitors. But unlike Brighton or Margate, the town remained quiet, which was precisely why I went there.

In the morning, while wandering towards the seaside near the station, I noticed many stalls at the seaside plaza where I had taken sunset photos the previous night. It was Sunday – a market day, and buyers and sellers were chatting like friends. If you liked something, you bought it. The prices of some small paintings shocked me. Their quality was subjective – if you liked it, it was worth it. I strolled around lazily until my eyes were drawn to a stall with sculptures. I stood still, mesmerised by the view. There were only a few "poorly made" sculptures on display, resembling open books with their pages twisted together. These sculptures were unique, requiring a special aesthetic to appreciate. There was no price tag, and I wouldn't buy one anyway, but I was captivated by the design. Next to the sculptures there were two long scroll-like architectural drawings displayed on an easel. It was still early, and not many people were around. The stall owner, dressed in red, greeted me warmly. I felt strangely drawn to and familiar with these three sculptures, as if re-encountering an old lover. I sensed a story behind them. Art and religion often cure loneliness. I followed the artist into the story of her sculptures. The sculptures were created for her husband, who had passed away 50 months ago, she whispered to me. Looking at the sculptures, I closed my eyes to better channel my emotions. I told her that the shape of the porcelain sculptures must have felt like touching her husband's skin. As I spoke about these tactile sensations, I could describe them with precision because it felt natural to do this when discussing beautiful things. The words came effortlessly, flowing directly from my lips in an unstoppable stream. She nodded excitedly, saying, "Exactly, it's the same as talking to my husband."

The outermost dark brown part of the sculptures was made from her husband's leather wallet, and the pages inside were taken from the Bible; her husband was a man of faith. I asked if she would be willing to part with these unique sculptures. She said, "Each time it's like a small exhibition; whether people buy them or not doesn't matter." To me, these weren't just sculptures; they were true art, representations of true love in life.

We often question the meaning of life in this world. How absurd is our repetitive and seemingly meaningless existence? Encountering this woman and hearing her story made me reflect. It brought me into close contact with kind people. She could recall precisely how many days her husband had been gone. Halfway through our conversation, she stepped aside to compose herself; possibly to cry. I asked if she lived nearby. She pointed to a row of boats in the distance, indicating her home – the largest houseboat at the far end. I asked if it would be convenient to stay the night, offering to pay to sleep on a bunk. She explained that the boat had two bedrooms and two bathrooms, one reserved for guests, and a large kitchen. Her husband had spent two and a half years building the houseboat, and though he was no longer with her, she continued to live in the harbour. That boat was like his body, always protecting her. She breathed him in with every drop of air.

The pursuit of love varies greatly between China and the West, though necessity remains a constant everywhere. A popular saying among young adults in China is, "I'd rather cry in a BMW than laugh on the back of a bicycle." It seems that materialism has overtaken everything, making genuine connections increasingly rare. Conversations often revolve around money, cars and houses. People compare the size of their home, its proximity to the city centre, or the brand of their cars. A friend of mine who had lived in Germany for years returned to Beijing to catch up with old friends, only to find both the conversations and the people she once knew had changed beyond recognition. If a marriage isn't based on love, it is destined to struggle. In the West, it's more common to see couples come together because they are soulmates.

At the place I stayed in Leigh-on-Sea, there was a large piece of artwork framed in delicate wood, hanging at the entrance. It marked the number of days the couple had spent together, up until the 6th of September, 2023. Though I only stayed two nights, it felt like a lifetime's lesson in happiness. The hosts spoke little, but rather immersed themselves in books. Love, for some, it seems, is not about wealth or possessions, but a carefully decorated home, a record of shared days, and time spent reading together.

Life has no definitive meaning, nor is there a right or wrong way to live. Life goes on, much like Sisyphus, endlessly pushing his boulder uphill. There is no winning or losing, no ultimate purpose or outcome. Nor should life's meaning be measured by any external scale. The meaning of life – if there is one – lies in finding possibility within the impossible, in continuing even when the fuel runs out. It's a difficult journey, one that demands positivity even in discomfort. But within that lies possibility. How can you see it unless you forge ahead? It's a daunting path, often swallowed by darkness, but standing at the summit, you realise that every effort has only made you stronger and you see light guiding your way on the distant horizon.

When you gaze at the earth and the sun, you are empowered to shoulder all difficulties. Only then do you realise you have truly lived in this world, driving away emptiness and absurdity. Temptations no longer trouble you. Living is the meaning of existence! Be it on the boat near the coast where a widowed woman honours her husband, or during my own slow journey of self-discovery, I found not only love but also a profound answer to my search for the meaning of life in these "small" yet significant sculptures.

About the author

Sun Hong (pen names: Zixiao, Sun Baiding) holds a master's degree in Museum Studies from the University of Leicester and a master's degree in Curating Cultures from SOAS, University of London. As a senior cultural and art lecturer, Sun Hong also volunteers for several museums and charitable organisations.

My British Husband, The Avid Runner

Written by: Yao Feiyan
Translated by: Yu Chen Luo

Established in London by an incredible Chinese man named He Yizhou and his friends, the club CUKRUN organised the first Chinese-arranged charity run in London in 2017. In support of this historically significant event, I brought my kids and husband Lao An to participate in this large-scale running race organised by the Chinese community.

As an amateur runner who has completed more than 10 marathons, Lao An breezed through the 10-kilometre run. However, when he went up to collect his award, the runner-up, a fellow Chinese man, stepped forward to challenge the result. "Impossible. He couldn't have come in first. I led the pack the entire way, and there was no one ahead of me!" It seemed that this lovely fellow might be barking up the wrong tree. From what I observed, Lao An dashed ahead like lightning, leaving him far behind. While I couldn't exactly recall how much faster Lao An was, it was clear that this skilled runner didn't even see the dust kicked up by Lao An.

Although Lao An took home the first-place prize, he was banned from participating in future races with my Chinese friends. His blazing speed put him in a league of his own. Now, he's only allowed to volunteer at Chinese-organised runs.

In Britain, running is practically a national sport. Whether in London or smaller towns, you'll spot people hitting the streets at dawn, dusk or even deep into the night for a run. Plenty also opt for a lunchtime jog. Brits typically get about an hour for lunch, where they grab a quick bite, sip on coffee and chat. Many enthusiasts squeeze in a run during this time.

Some prefer hitting the treadmill at the gym. But there's an ironic twist: in the 19th century, British prisoners were sentenced to eight hours of treadmill torture as punishment. In 1818, Sir William Cubitt, an English engineer, invented the first treadmill. Prisoners had to continuously step on a large wheel or risk falling off. By the late 19th century, the British deemed this punishment too cruel and abolished it. Later on, the Americans patented the idea, and it's now a global phenomenon.

Yet a significant portion of Brits still prefer outdoor running. Throughout the UK, you'll find events like 5Ks, 10Ks, half marathons and full marathons happening year-round. On weekends, there are park runs where hundreds of people from nearby villages gather to run 5K. There are also charity runs like GoodGym. People enjoy being charitable while running through the scenic British countryside.

Whether it's freezing cold, windy or raining, Lao An is outside running. He has clocked up thousands of kilometres wearing a no-drills pair of shorts and a tank top, paired with fancy running shoes. He usually leaves his phone, headphones and other gadgets behind. No music or electronic watches are needed. He just loves the freedom of running.

But here's the kicker: he never takes picturesque, romantic runs. Instead, it's more common for him to return home covered in mud from a fall, or limping due to an accidental slip into a rabbit hole or molehill. If you look closely at his eyes, you'll see mosquitoes trapped in his eye sockets. To top things off, he'd often return home carrying a bag of trash, smelling of sweat and garbage. This is not the kind of running most Asians can imagine doing!

Lao An runs like the wind, but my stubby legs can't keep up. To match his pace, I resort to a mountain bike, and even then, barely manage to keep up. As Lao An enjoys picking up litter while jogging, both of his hands and my bike's handlebars are usually adorned with various plastic bags after an hour with him. That's why I can't have him tagging along whenever I yearn for a bike ride in the forest! Even thinking about taking a leisurely beach stroll with Lao An requires careful consideration. During our beach holiday in Thailand, he insisted on running along the shore every morning. Over time, I've become accustomed to watching his carefree figure dash off and return drenched in sweat, clutching a heap of garbage in his hands. Seeing how much he enjoys it, I can't help but shake my head and smile with fondness.

About the author

Yao Feiyan graduated from Peking University with a double major in information management and economics. In 2002, she pursued her studies at the London School of Economics and Political Science (LSE). Following her graduation, Yanfei spent nearly twenty years working in research and development management roles in the fields of computer technology and telecommunications at various multinational corporations. Concurrently, she pursued further studies in Telecommunications Engineering, Education and International Chinese Education at Queen Mary University of London, University of Cambridge and Jinan University. In recent years, Yanfei transitioned into the role of an education consultant, focusing on organising social practice activities and community service for young people, all while maintaining a commitment to holistic education.

Roam in the UK

Travel in the younger sort, is a part of education;
in the elder a part of experience.

Francis Bacon
Of Travel

What is "Posh"?

Written by: Yu Shan
Translated by: Chen Lin

I didn't even know the word "posh" existed when I first went to study abroad. The first time I heard it was from a British gentleman at Robinson College of Cambridge University. He was one year my senior and one of those keen and seasoned members of the postgraduate community who were happy to look after newbies. During one of our conversations, I was struggling to find an English word to describe something sophisticated in a Chinese context. Words like "best", "super good" and "high-class" felt inadequate, and I couldn't settle on the right term. Sensing my frustration, he seemed to read my mind and exclaimed, "Posh!" He then gave me some examples: the royal accent is posh, and luxurious items are also posh.

Later, a British postdoc named Mike from my department spotted me unpacking some biscuits – perhaps not as carefully as I thought. I meticulously removed the packaging, folding it neatly to create a square cover for the unfinished snacks. This was an ordinary habit for me, but it caught Mike's attention. He examined how perfectly it was done, then looked up at me and said, "That is posh!" I was both amazed and amused.

Growing up in a small village, I was fortunate that my mother made the extra effort to send me to junior high school in a larger town. We didn't have enough English teachers when English became a mandatory subject, so the headmaster had to borrow some from other schools. These teachers went to great lengths just to be there for us, only to return to their own schools after our classes. Despite their dedication, we were not particularly gifted students; only two out of more than fifty of us passed the exam. I didn't have a talent for humanities or for languages – I even stumbled in daily conversations. No method or technique seemed to improve my Chinese, let alone my English. I made a tremendous effort learning English in high school and university, relying on rote memorisation, repetition and a knack for passing exams to scrape through the College English Test. I remember getting the lowest possible mark needed to get into Cambridge as an international student. When I accepted my Cambridge offer and decided to study abroad, I booked a one-way flight from Shanghai to London. At that time, I didn't even know that "sour" and "sore" had different meanings until a fellow student from China clued me in and had a good laugh about this. But this was just a minor example of my bumpy journey to learn English. Some of the embarrassment caused by my mistakes in expression was particularly hard to describe.

Thankfully, during the first year of my PhD, Helen, a British postdoc in the lab taught me many English words and expressions out of pure kindness without ever asking for anything in return. That included patiently and candidly explaining some swear words to me that made my jaw drop. Everyone soon realised how limited my vocabulary was, and how little I knew about the profane world – I was an introverted student in an ivory tower. Rachel, a technician in my department, even gave me a hilarious Christmas gift: a dictionary of English swear words. My English has greatly improved after three years of hard work, and it continues to get better as my children grow. I now have my own understanding of the word "posh".

On Thursday, May 23rd, 2013, Queen Elizabeth II took a train to Cambridge for the launch of a new establishment at the Laboratory of Molecular Biology. Many were captivated by the royal event, going through the motions of work with our minds focused on the royal visit. Only a few people remained focused on their tasks, and I was one of them. Even though my experimental data was selected to be presented to Her Majesty, I couldn't abandon my experiment to see where the Queen was. The event organisers had turned the bathroom and pantry right next to our lab into a lounge for the Queen and her husband. These two rooms were cleaned and adorned with cream curtains trimmed with lace. Instantly, the humble pantry and restroom became "posh".

It took me some time to realise that in the UK, anything associated with royalty is considered posh. Some people think that handmade, artisanal products are posh. Others define posh as things into which they've invested their own efforts and thoughts. For example, vegetables they grow at home or drinks garnished with mint leaves from their own gardens, or loofah sponges made from gourds planted in the spring and harvested in the autumn.

Some British have even started to think that turning on the stove to make a hot meal for lunch is posh, given that they are so used to cold bread and sandwiches. There is also a relatively small population that considers posh things to be those that cost a fortune.

Living between Chinese and British cultures, my idea of posh differs from all of these. Every individual has, and should have, their own understanding of what posh means. To me, having a free life is the real posh. The ability to make various choices at will is true poshness. It is essentially a right granted by personal effort and social progress, and it belongs to everyone – a right to choose: to build a family and have children, or to live freely and alone; to pursue education until nothing more is offered, or to leave school and start a business; to be a supportive family member, or to focus wholeheartedly on a career. Ultimately, it is the right to spend every precious minute and every valuable second as we see fit. In my view, the more options we have, the more powerful we become, and the posher we are.

About the author

Yu Shan was born in Zhejiang, China, and has a PhD from the PhD, Department of Pathology, Cambridge University. Yu Shan has over a decade of experience in laboratory virus studies and is currently a Cambridge researcher funded by the Royals Foundation. She served as a researcher at the Medical Research Council, Laboratory of Molecular Biology (LMB), and left in 2014 to be a full-time mother, suspending her research work for nearly a decade. In 2020-21, she worked for the Milton Keynes Lighthouse Laboratory and contributed to Cambridge University's efforts during the COVID-19 pandemic. Yu Shan currently lives in Cambridge where she writes, and shares her life stories in her free time.

British Accents

Written by: He Kai
Translated by: Veronica Wong

The British accent is like a box of Bertie Bott's Every Flavour Beans from the magical *Harry Potter* universe. You never know which flavour your ears will encounter when walking down the street.

When I first arrived in the UK, I was eager for my ears to immerse themselves in pure, authentic British tones. Instead, I discovered a different reality. Travelling from southern England to Scotland, if I managed to avoid saying "pardon?" less than ten times a day, it felt like a minor miracle. Even in London, it was hard to make out what people were saying. Over time, I've gotten used to the diversity of British accents, but I still feel unprepared and surprised whenever I run into an unfamiliar one.

In the world of English, there is no equivalent to Mandarin, which serves as a standard spoken Chinese language for people from all parts of China. The English we hear in school in China, or from TV series or films is typically known as Received Pronunciation (RP), mainly spoken by the British middle and upper classes. It is often mistaken for the London accent, which is revered by Chinese people. As a senior member of the International Phonetic Association, I teach English pronunciation and correct students' accents. Many of them are desperate to learn the "London accent", and I always need to help them distinguish between RP or Cockney. Cockney is the working-class accent of London, particularly from the East End. One of its key features is the strong glottal stop, like the word "better" should be pronounced as /ˈbeʔə/ with the /t/ sound omitted. Its coarse pronunciation and disregard for grammatical nuances once marked it as the speech of the lower classes, quite the opposite of RP.

RP is associated with prestige and the upper classes. Many prime ministers are die-hard RP enthusiasts. The BBC also played a crucial role in promoting this refined accent with its news anchors articulating it fluently. As Lu Xun, a famous Chinese writer once said, "There were no roads to begin with, but when many people pass one way, a road is made."

Historically, regional British accents in the UK co-existed like states during the Warring States period in China: each carved out their own turf in the British Isles and was content with it. Since the early 19th century, however, the meteoric rise of RP seemed to promise the unification of the fragmented landscape of duchies under a single powerful duke. In the 20th century, the winds changed. Social norms changed, diversity was embraced and other British accents entered the limelight. The Beatles, for example, with their heavy Liverpudlian accents, became global icons.

Even William, Prince of Wales, has a different accent from Charles III and Elizabeth II – his is less posh and closer to the common British accent. Perhaps the royal family recognises that tradition matters, but openness and diversity are the keys to survival.

Living in the UK, you will discover a vibrant symphony when talking to people from different regions. Everyone has unique pronunciations, intonations, stresses and rhythms. Over time, I have developed a talent for identifying someone's origin solely by their voice. Each accent carries its own distinct flavour and your ears can binge on a feast of accents when wandering the street. These varied sounds breathe life into conversations.

Reflecting on my life growing up speaking Mandarin, I have nearly forgotten my native dialect. We use Mandarin for everything – during work, school, dating and even swearing. As we've embraced a homogenous accent for the sake of easy communication, we've lost the flavor and humour of our distinctive local dialects.

In the UK, British accents mirror society. Just as different social classes sometimes clash and fight, they can also work together and thrive. Even though the upper class establishes the standard, others do not have to follow it. RP might be considered the mainstream, but people are free to speak in their own accents and still find their place in society. After all, language exists for interaction and communication. It's what we say to each other that matters most.

About the author

He Kai is a Fellow of the Royal Society of Arts, a Fellow of the Royal Asiatic Society, a chartered linguist, an official collaborator with the Royal College of Music, a senior member of the International Phonetic Association, a bilingual poet and lyricist, and a literary translator.

Right to Roam

Written by: Zhang Ye
Translated by: Seth O'Farrell

British people have peculiar rights. For example, the British have the right to sunlight entering their home from their windows (right to light), so homeowners whose light is blocked by their neighbour's houses often launch lawsuits. Similarly, British customers have the right to get free tap water from anywhere with a liquor licence (tap water right). When they go to a pub, they can ask the waiter to fill their water bottle with tap water (although the latter has the right to charge for filtered water). The British also have the right to roam in special terrains such as mountains, swamps and grasslands, even if the land is private property.

When I first arrived in the UK, I thought this "right to roam" was inconceivable.

As a Chinese city girl, it is hard to imagine under what circumstances one might roam across other people's land. The roads in my hometown were always perfectly straight: streets with eight car lanes ran across the city from all points of the compass. The process of getting from one point to another was numerical: you drove in one direction and turned when you needed to. If you turned too soon or too late, there could be dire consequences. I remember once my dad and I parked a block away from our destination. At first, I was secretly delighted that we had found a good parking spot but didn't realise that we would have to walk for forty five minutes in the glacial December winter winds before reaching our destination. In this kind of special environment, I learned how to survive getting from one point to another in the fastest way possible. This kind of knowledge came to be of unprecedented value when I left school to go to university. After adding up the time spent studying for two degrees, one week's worth of classes consumed forty hours from Monday to Sunday. Then outside of classes I had exams and extracurricular activities. Just going from the dormitory to the classrooms took half an hour. So whether I was rushing for an early class at 8am or dashing to the canteen for a coveted spot at lunch, it was critical for me to be able to leave the dormitory at exactly the right time and find a yellow Ofo bike in exactly the right place so I could ride to my destination at breakneck speed.

I used to think that this kind of survival knowledge would serve me for life. But life brings about unexpected changes. When I arrived in London, there were no longer dormitories enclosed by towering school walls, nor any yellow Ofo bikes. Walking was the only option. London's small roads criss-cross: it is common to see five roads extending down from one small hill in all directions. Not to mention, said roads frequently twist and turn into dead ends. And so, even with the help of modern technology such as Google Maps, it's impossible to navigate with precision. Even if you manage to avoid getting lost and recover ten minutes by making every second count, you can't use it to work non-stop, like I thought I should. After arriving at my laboratory, I would often boil some water to make tea in the communal kitchen. I'd chat with my colleagues for a few minutes, and then slip away. They'd stay behind, talking about their weekends – a concert in Scotland, a visit home to see parents. My weekends were always spent working. In fact, my supervisors were so tired of receiving emails from me during out-of-office hours that they gave me explicit and implicit requests to take the weekends off.

All of a sudden, my winning strategy of racing against time seemed to have turned me into a sad person with no social life. A new environment requires new knowledge, and luckily, I was smart enough to embrace both. I met my then-boyfriend and now husband for our first date one December afternoon. We had planned to go to the Grand Union Canal in Camden, which was only a ten-minute walk from Kings Cross Station, near where I lived.

London in December is often overcast and rainy but on that day the weather was fantastic. The sun shone on the water's surface, reflecting glimmering lights underneath the dark coloured stone bridges, while the long shadows of different shades were cast on dark green moss. As a group of five dust-coloured Canadian geese swam by, my date told me that the group of five geese were probably a family, and that they'd stay in a group no matter what. As we made our way along the river, we walked for twenty minutes or so and came upon Camden's Stable Market. I was surprised to discover that Camden was one of the most hip and humble areas in London's centre. Its stalls contained everything from snacks and coffee to second-hand books, antique tableware and gothic clothing. In one Egyptian souvenir shop, the shopkeeper and my now husband, an Egyptologist, were engaged in such lively conversation that business was put on hold for at least half an hour. Even though we didn't buy anything, the shopkeeper very kindly offered me a turquoise scarab as a gift. I was flattered by this act of kindness but also slightly worried for this man, as he seemed like someone who was here to make friends instead of money. There is a bronze statue of Amy Winehouse outside the Stable Market. While reading the description, I realised that when she died, Winehouse was living in Camden. All of this was only 30 minutes from where I lived, but after three months in London, I was only now discovering it. It's as if I had entered a new world. I had to see what else was out there.

My husband and I bought a London walking guidebook which became a weekly weekend activity for us. We'd pick one of the 25 routes in the book at random and set off, learning fascinating things along the way. For instance, Hitler's cousin once lived in Soho on 4 Percy Street and Hitler himself even came to visit him in 1912. In Farringdon, there's a church called St Etheldreda's. It looks unassuming from the outside, but actually contains a massive, magnificent stained glass window that covers an entire wall. It's one of England's oldest churches, built early in the thirteenth century.

Ironically, one of the most interesting discoveries was my place of work, where I spent night and day: 26 Bedford Way. It was a deep grey concrete building. I prefer Georgian and Victorian houses, so I had never given the exterior much attention until one on one of our walks I learned that it was an outstanding example of 20th century brutalist architecture.

We walked around London like this for two years, and there were days when we'd be out for 12 hours and rack up as many as 40,000 steps. I even got a new epithet from my friends "Walks far!" I was pleased with this new identity.

Little did I know, I was still earning my walking stripes.

One spring, my husband and I went on holiday to Bath. When we left the city to go to Prior Park, Google Maps suggested a busy motorway. Since it was not scenic, my husband and I opted for an ordinary-looking small road on the map instead. Unexpectedly, this small road was not an ordinary city alleyway but a public footpath. Nine times out of ten, a public footpath is a dirt road with bushes and thickets. It had rained a few days before, so the ground was wet and muddy, but it was too late to turn back. As I saw other walkers with windproof clothing, hiking boots and poles, I looked down at my own suit, coat and little white shoes and couldn't help but say to them: "You're very well-equipped."

It was then I realised that walking in the English countryside has its own set of tricks. When we lived in the small town of Amersham on the outskirts of London, my husband and I splurged on a whole new wardrobe of country clothes and country shoes. Once we had this kit, we blended in perfectly with the old ramblers and wandered from village to village along the public footpaths with the locals. At that time, I had been living in London for six years and thought of myself as half local. But like the first time I discovered Camden Market, I was surprised to find another world not that far away. A narrow path would sometimes follow a creek and lead into a dense forest as the sunlight, splintered by the trees, would fall on thick mottled leaves. But once you got through the forest, vast fields would open up in front of you, as far as the eye could see. It all looked like a desktop from Windows XP!

During my walks I picked up indispensable bits of knowledge about leaves being trimmed with frozen silver after a frost, or about how etiquette requires one to smile and greet a fellow passing hiker. It was on a hike that I tried my first Sunday roast in a village pub and discovered a small church built in the Anglo-Saxon period that contained Norman murals.

My husband and I became walking experts. I could chat for hours in pubs with friends who were born and bred in the UK about all the little fun things to do in small British towns. In the end, they would give me an admiring look, saying that my knowledge of the UK was roughly akin to that of the locals. It was then I realised that all these years I had been making use of the British "right to roam", by roaming across other people's land and enjoying it. Roaming became one of my life's greatest hobbies. In the city or the country, on large streets or in small alleys, I realised that if you just slow down and pay attention, everywhere has a story.

In the unremarkable Markfield Park in Haringey, just outside of London's city centre, there is a nineteenth-century steam engine. On specific days of every year, it gets switched on by aspiring engineers. It huffs and it puffs, and it breathes life into a long gone era. In springtime on the East Hill of Hastings, there are fresh, bright yellow flowers, reflecting the deep blues of the sea and sky in the distance. There is an interesting town in Kent called Wye (yes, it sounds like "why"): and outside of the town there is a very long, narrow climbing path that goes along a nature reserve. At a magical point on the path, the landscape opens up into a sea of glistening green.

The year we went to Bath, we bought a guidebook written by an architect. As an architect, the writer denounced a newly-built straight and wide road as ugly, "This is not a street, it's a route." I couldn't help but remember the large streets and small alleys I rode through at breakneck speed during my calculated youth. Regardless of the beauty of the landscape, everything was just a route to me – a way to get from A to B in the most efficient way possible. Fortunately, I've since learned that an unexamined life is not worth living and I never leave home without my passport to roam.

About the author

Dr. Zhang Ye is a data scientist with a background in cognitive neuroscience. Her dream is to one day roam along the Via Francigena all the way to Rome.

home

Sending Letters Home from Red Postboxes

Written by: Aurora Wang

Upon arrival in the UK, one is often captivated by the sight of red postboxes lining the streets. Some say that the red signifies urgency, showcasing the efficiency of the British postal system. Others say that the royal association with red denotes nobility, and the British populace simply favours it as a primary colour. There are even those who think that red symbolises the sincere and passionate emotions of the letter-writers. However, in reality, when postboxes were first introduced to Britain in 1840, they were not the iconic deep red we know today but were painted a deep green. Due to public complaints that the deep green postboxes blended into the rainy and foggy London weather, making them hard to see and leading to collisions with pedestrians and cyclists, the Post Office decided to repaint them a bright red. This charming incident highlights a delightful aspect of the British character.

Today, the UK boasts a delightful array of postbox designs, from the classic cylindrical style to wall-mounted versions, illuminated boxes, and even those shaped like animated characters. It's as if the postboxes are strutting down a fashion runway, each with its own unique flair. Furthermore, postboxes are no longer limited to just one colour. During the 2012 London Olympics, for every gold medal won, the Royal Mail painted a postbox in the champion's hometown gold and kept it that way permanently. Moreover, the upper half of the front of a postbox features a date plaque and an information card, akin to a time machine, indicating the next collection date for letters and contact details for nearby post offices. The lower half of the postbox typically bears a large crown and letters representing the period in which the postbox was established; for example, "E||R" indicates that the postbox was set up during the reign of Queen Elizabeth II, reminiscent of the inscriptions found on some antiques in museums, such as "Made during the Yongzheng reign of the Great Qing Dynasty" or "Made during the Qianlong reign of the Great Qing Dynasty."

While pursuing my postgraduate studies in the UK, I found myself drawn to these red postboxes, which always reminded me of the times I used to help my mother read and write letters as a child. I often imagined myself slipping a letter into one of these antique-like postboxes and sending it to my mother. However, it wasn't until after graduating from postgraduate school that I finally sent her a postcard through one of the red postboxes. It took two months for the postcard to reach her hands. Perhaps it was the long wait, or perhaps it was the first time she received an expression of love from her daughter, but when she finished reading the postcard, my mother cried. She reflected that the days when I, as a little child, helped her read letters from distant relatives felt like just yesterday. Yet, in the blink of an eye, I had grown into someone who writes to her from even further away. And in that moment, she realised that this distance might be a place she would never reach in her lifetime.

I come from a small rural village in southern Xinjiang, China. As a child, the moment I looked forward to the most every week was Thursday at noon, when the postman arrived at school on his motorcycle, carrying a dark green mailbag. Among the stack of letters he delivered, I would eagerly search for those from my aunts and uncles in Gansu. When I brought them home, I would read them to my mother again and again. The letters were filled with everyday anecdotes from distant relatives, along with their care and greetings for my mother. They were simple and sincere sentences, but to this day, they remain the most beloved and unforgettable words I have ever read. Since my mother never attended school, I would write the replies for her. After composing the letters, we would mail them together at the county post office and eagerly await a response. Sometimes, our distant relatives would also send along little gifts with their letters, and my mother has carefully preserved everything, both the letters and the accompanying items. Later, within just four or five years, telephones and smartphones became increasingly common in China, and I stopped reading or writing letters for my mother, until I encountered the ubiquitous red postboxes that dot the streets and alleys of Britain.

In the UK, the culture of letters and cards feels like a delightful party, full of surprises at every turn. In addition to the iconic red postboxes, the "card corner" in major supermarkets is a hidden gem waiting to be explored. Here, you can find a wide array of cards for every occasion imaginable, from birthdays and holidays to anniversaries. There are cards specifically designed for parents' wedding anniversaries and others commemorating things as specific as a friend's achievement in passing their driving test.

But it doesn't stop there! Within each specific role-related card category, there are further subdivisions based on various scenarios. For example, cards related to daughters can be categorised as daughter, daughter's first Christmas, and daughter's first to 21st birthdays (after turning 21, it's mostly milestone birthday cards), as well as step-daughter, god-daughter, daughter and her partner, daughter and her girlfriend, daughter and son-in-law, and so on. Cards related to sons are similarly subdivided. After buying and writing the cards, you can seal them in envelopes, affix stamps and drop them in the postbox, or simply take them to the post office for mailing. This traditional culture of letter-writing is filled with joy and warmth, adding a lot of happiness and emotional exchange to people's lives.

Additionally, the postal system in the UK is highly developed. It's like an invisible hero silently supporting the entire country's way of life.

In the UK, almost all documents, bank cards, bills, and even passports, BRP (Biometric Residence Permit) cards, etc., are delivered through the postal service. The modern postal system and the concept of postage stamps originated in the UK, with the world's first postage stamp, the "Penny Black", being issued in 1840 – a true British masterpiece. Actually, long before the British postal system began using stamps, letter-writing had already become a part of people's lives. However, the difference was that before 1840, writing letters in the UK wasn't a wallet-friendly affair. During the time of renowned writers like Jane Austen (1775–1817), postage was determined by factors such as the weight, distance and quantity of the letters, often paid by the recipient. Therefore, letter writers had to ensure their content was concise and valuable; otherwise, the recipient might feel uneasy about being charged for the letter. Austen herself was a masterful communicator, with every word in her letters being a thoughtful gift. Upon receiving letters, Austen praised the sender for their articulate, concise and clear writing style, which also reflected her own. Austen was born into a poor but loving family and was once engaged to a young man named Tom Lefroy, but they ultimately broke up due to their poverty. In a letter to her sister, Austen wrote, "Friday – I and Tom Lefroy had our last meeting of love. By the time you read this letter, everything will be over – as I write, my heart is full of sadness, tears gushing like a fountain." From that time on, Austen began writing the epistolary novel *Elinor and Marianne*, which served as the precursor to *Sense and Sensibility*.

In recent years, with the development of the "fast but not broken" internet era, our connections with family and friends have become increasingly convenient, and the days of waiting for letters seem to be fading away. As Chinese writer Mu Xin said, "The days of the past have become slow, with slow cars, slow horses, and slow mail." The care and blessings found in handwritten letters from a slower-paced life, the sincerity and warmth revealed in everyday greetings, and the lingering aftertaste that can be savoured time and again – all these, along with the imagined surprise when the recipient receives the letter or the joy of finally getting a reply after a long wait, are truly irreplaceable. The red postboxes in Britain serve as gentle guardians, quietly standing on the streets and continually reminding passers-by that while they enjoy the convenience of a fast-paced life, they can also take a moment to savour the exquisite and warm moments nurtured by attentiveness. It's an invitation to slow down and earnestly cultivate those precious feelings.

About the author

Aurora Wang is a volunteer at the Mothers' Bridge of Love (London Headquarters) and literature enthusiast, obtained a master's degree in Education from the University of Leeds in 2023.

My Stories of Edinburgh

Written by: Zhang Heruijie

1. Windy Edinburgh

"Edinburgh is very windy!", or so have I warned all of my friends who came to Edinburgh to visit. But I guess the word "windy" just does not carry enough meaning because all of my friends, one after another, insisted on using an umbrella in Edinburgh and all ended up lamenting how the wind destroyed their umbrellas. I could relate, as I too once lost a beloved umbrella to the winds of Edinburgh.

Before coming to the UK, I used to care a lot about my appearance. But after just two weeks in Edinburgh, I gave up on combing my hair altogether. Instead, I'd simply run my fingers through it a couple of times and step outside, leaving the task of styling to the most renowned hairdresser in the city – Miss Wind. After all, in Edinburgh, your hair often ends up looking like a flag billowing in the breeze, so really, what's the point of fussing over it?

I remember when I first came to Edinburgh, I was ignorant and fearless, utterly unafraid of the wind. I went out with two friends on an especially windy day, and it is still one of my most "moving and tragic" memories.

I found myself in the middle, my right arm wrapped tightly around my friend's left, while she clung to a sturdy street pole as if her life depended on it. Her right hand was gripping her clothes so fiercely that it seemed as though, if she let go, the wind might rip her coat – and her skin – right off, leaving only a cartoonish skeleton behind. On my left, I was holding onto another friend, who was much too skinny for the battle we were facing. The wind filled her eyes with tears, and we locked gazes. If this were a film, she would've whispered, "One of us has to survive," before dramatically letting go of my hand, tears streaming down her face. I'd be left standing there, watching as she tumbled down the hill, blown all the way from the city centre to the sea. Luckily, after half an hour of fighting the wind, we reached our destination in one piece – with our clothes and skin intact.

Relax, it is usually not this windy in Edinburgh.

2. Sunset at Calton Hill

Calton Hill, situated to the east of Princes Street, is one of Edinburgh's most famous viewpoints. Many of the city's iconic pictures and paintings are captured from this little hill. It holds a special place in my heart, as I've witnessed countless beautiful sunsets there with friends. Sometimes, while walking towards Princes Street, we'd change our minds and head to Calton Hill instead. We'd try to snag a bench with the best view, sitting side by side, our legs swinging back and forth like children. We'd complain about endless assignments and readings, share moments of happiness or worry from our lives, and indulge in the latest juicy gossip we'd picked up.

The sunsets were always stunning. Sometimes, they cast a reddish-orange glow, like the morning sun or the gentle flame of a hearth, softly yet majestically crowning Edinburgh. Other times, the sky turned a yellowish-orange, reminiscent of the warm light on a porch welcoming you home after a long journey. My favourite, though, was the rare pink sunset. It was like a little girl in a pink dress with hints of blue, shyly waving goodbye, disappearing in the blink of an eye.

On clear days, Calton Hill attracted a crowd of people, much like my friend and I, drawn by a whim to sit on the benches or sprawl on the grass. Laughter and chatter filled the air, and dogs ran freely – some chasing after balls their humans threw, while others mingled with the crowd, waiting for anyone to pat them on the head and exclaim, "Aww, so cute!"

There was also the famous, unfinished structure that looked like a dilapidated Parthenon. It wasn't actually in ruins – only half the money had been raised to complete it. Perhaps because of this, most Edinburgh locals showed little reverence for it, turning "how to climb up the 160cm-high platform of the temple" into a popular game. I suspected that my height and biceps wouldn't allow me to climb up gracefully, so I never tried. Neither did my friend, who always accompanied me to Calton Hill. But we both enjoyed watching others make the attempt. Whenever someone hoisted themselves up, pressing their hands on the top of the platform, swinging a leg over, and effortlessly standing up, we'd clap from a distance, cheering, "10 out of 10!"

3. Deep-fried Mars Bars

Mars Bars, as most know, are a popular sweet treat – a milk chocolate bar filled with caramel and nougat. But leave it to a fish and chips restaurant in Scotland to take this ordinary treat and elevate (or perhaps complicate) it into something new: the *deep-fried Mars Bar*. The process is straightforward – coat the bar in a thick layer of batter and fry it until it turns a golden brown. Serve it with a scoop of vanilla ice cream, and voilà, a dessert is born.

When you eat it, the ritual begins. You take a spoonful of ice cream alongside a piece of the battered Mars Bar. The ice cream melts in your mouth, cooling you down. Then, the crunchy fried shell cracks open, and the melted chocolate, caramel and nougat come rushing in. The ice cream softens the overwhelming sweetness of the chocolate and tempers the greasiness of the fried shell. It's a battle of contrasts – hot and cold, crispy and gooey – all blending together in your mouth.

I've tried deep fried Mars bars twice, and yet I remain undecided. Each bite prompted me to analyse its taste as if I were solving a puzzle. One Scottish classmate offered an interesting perspective, saying it tastes best when you're drunk. Perhaps it's because, in that state, you'd no longer care to question whether it's good or bad – you just enjoy it.

4. Bibi's Bakery

Initially, I proclaimed that Bibi's Bakery had "the world's best macaron". However, not all my friends shared my enthusiasm; some even suggested it didn't quite live up to the hype. So, I adjusted my approach, saying it was "the best macaron I have ever tasted". This way, if anyone disagreed, they might simply think of me as a naïve country bumpkin who hadn't experienced finer things in life. And honestly, I'm quite happy to embrace that persona for the sake of this bakery.

My love for macarons has led me to sample them from various shops. Typically, these tiny delights come in just a few standard flavours – chocolate, vanilla or strawberry. Some shops may boast a wider array of flavours, but in reality, they often taste remarkably similar. The macarons are often lined up inside a glass counter, each with a price tag that boldly declares, "I don't care if you buy me or not."

The first time I saw Bibi's Bakery, I was drawn in by its charm. The shop featured two glass walls showcasing an array of colourful cupcakes and macarons. As I stepped inside, I was mesmerised by the mountains of desserts, only to realise, after a moment, that they were merely models. The real macarons were delicately arranged in glass containers atop the counter, forming charming little pine-cone-shaped piles. Each day offered a different selection of flavours: salted caramel, pistachio, cherry, and my all-time favourite – violet. Each flavour was distinct; even with my eyes closed, I could identify them immediately.

Every macaron was meticulously decorated. Even the simplest designs featured gold or silver sprinkles, all of them cheerfully beckoning, "Hi! How do we look? Do you like us?" And I did! I would buy them in boxes, carrying my precious macarons home at a brisk pace, unable to contain my excitement to devour them.

Many macarons I'd tried in the past were excessively sweet, leaving me unable to eat more than two. But Bibi's were different. I could easily devour an entire box, seven pieces at a time. What I adored most was the generous layer of filling between the crispy shells, which required a bit of chewing rather than just melting away. Perhaps this wasn't how "fancy" macarons were meant to taste, but it certainly left me feeling satisfied.

As I write this article, I've discovered that Bibi's Bakery has closed its doors permanently. I'll never again experience the anticipation, excitement and satisfaction I felt during those monthly visits over my four years in Edinburgh. What remains are these short paragraphs, a bittersweet reminder of those wonderful times. So don't wait – before another beautiful shop disappears, go visit Edinburgh!

About the author

Zhang Heruijie is a freelance translator and interpreter with a Bachelor's degree in Linguistics from the University of Edinburgh and a master's degree in Translation and Interpreting from the University of Bath.

Birdwatching

Written by: Cao Tingting
Translated by: Yao Gong

Standing in the corner of the courtyard, half raising my head and staring at the pale blue sky, I tried to keep as still as possible. Birds have such a keen sense of sight that they must have already been aware of my presence, but they were too preoccupied to care A fierce battle between two blackbirds and a sparrowhawk was raging on in mid-air, with both sides dashing high and low. I watched, breathless and completely mesmerised by the spectacle.

I was not sure which side would win. The female sparrowhawk knew the neighborhood well. The other day, she was seen perching quietly on a nearby fence, a small, already lifeless, purple-winged starling clutched in her sharp talons. The moment she took off into the sky, a light greyish-brown feather with cinnamon edges was left in her wake. Out of nowhere, an adult starling with purple wings darted down and cried out mournfully at the feather. She had just lost her baby.

The sparrowhawk reappeared the following day, but this time it encountered joint resistance by two female blackbirds committed to protecting their nestlings. They didn't have the strength to fight with the female sparrowhawk alone, so they flew in a circle around it, up and down, left and right, risking their lives. They managed to peck the sparrowhawk on its front and rear. Overwhelmed, it finally stumbled from the air and staggered along the ground It stretched its wings to regain its composure, then rushed back up into the air and flew away.

Several years ago when I first came to England, I visited a senior physics professor. He solemnly told me that birdwatching had been his lifelong hobby. I was puzzled. In my very limited understanding of birdwatching, I thought it was something that should be conducted by professionals. Can bird-spotting on a casual stroll merit serious discussion? Indeed it can.

The origins of birdwatching can be traced back to the scientific study of birds in the 18th century. At that time, the wealthy hunted birds to make specimens for their collections. As the study of the natural history of birds progressed, however, the practice of killing birds was under scrutiny. In the late 18th century, the English naturalist Gilbert White began observing birds in their natural habitats and recording their behaviours. His book, *The Natural History of Selborne*, is considered a classic in the field of ornithology. British ornithologist Edmund Selous coined the term "bird-watching" and contributed to popularising the practice of observing birds in their natural habitats. By the 20th century, birdwatching had become a widespread hobby.

The UK is not only the birthplace of birdwatching, but it is a hobby that is encouraged and benefits from many active communities. There are suitable birdwatching activities for everyone from veteran birdwatchers to beginners.

And so, I began paying more mind to birds. I discovered and entirely new world of crows pecking at the sacrifices left at temples and pigeons roaming the traditional old Chinese alleyways known as hutongs – Those birds, once animated by Chinese poets for centuries, have now flown into my world in a foreign land. When travelling home to visit my family, I discovered "new" birds in familiar parks from time to time. It was only when I looked them up that I realised that they had been living in this area all along; I just hadn't paid attention to them before.

With a history of more than 100 years, the Royal Society for the Protection of Birds (RSPB) is one of the world's largest wildlife conservation organisations. It has branched out into many local groups, encompassing and maintaining over two hundred nature reserves. In order to cultivate an awareness of the protection of birds and respect for nature, the RSPB has organised the Big Garden Birdwatch every January. During this event, people from all corners of the country are encouraged to birdwatch and register their sightings in a centralised database. The result is Britain's largest garden wildlife survey, which attracts close to a million people each year. The data collected on the distribution of bird populations, ecological changes and migration timing patterns also helps scientists and ornithologists understand the impact of human activity and climate change on birds and their habitats.

This event always receives extensive coverage from the media. As I witnessed the great enthusiasm for it, I had an epiphany. The British have produced some of the best nature documentaries in the world. This is all the result of generous financial investment, years of experience, cutting-edge equipment and an undying love for nature. Sir David Attenborough, the world-renowned father of nature documentaries, has shown a deep curiosity for nature since childhood. His family and community encouraged him to explore the wonders of natural life with an undiminished passion. I hope that some of Britain's young birdwatchers will follow in his footsteps and continue to document the awe-inspiring world above us.

About the author

Cao Tingting, an electronic engineer now living in Cambridge, UK, is the head of The Arts Society Cambridge, a member of the European Immigrant Chinese Writers' Association and the art director of *European Immigrant Chinese Poets*. Her essays, poems, and commentaries can be seen in *Chinese Monthly*, *Women Too*, *River Cam Breeze*, *Chinese Poetry Garden*, and other literary magazines. She has published the collection *A New and Colorful Scroll*, *Floating Clouds*, *Where the Heart Lies*, among others.

A Spot of Tea

Written by: Xiangyu
Translated by: Wuyi

Imagine a summer's day in England, where the sky is clear, the light is perfect, and the temperature is just right. Beneath a wisteria-draped tree, a round table is draped in a beautifully embroidered tablecloth, and adorned with fresh flowers and gleaming tea sets. Imagine sitting there, with no worries or concerns; just pleasant idle chatter among female friends. There is no need to think about Monday or household chores, or the endless to-do list at work. This small slice of afternoon tea time slips through the fingers like delicate sand. Another Sunday afternoon drifts away, leaving a touch of contentment tinged with melancholy.

This idyllic scene described above took place in the charming garden of an old friend in Cambridge. We spent our time sipping tea and admiring flowers, the memories of which remain vivid and warm as if they have quietly been preserved into the amber of time.

In England, traditional afternoon tea is usually served between 3:00 and 5:00 in the afternoon. In hotels or tea gardens, it comes with specialty black tea and a traditional three-tier stand: a selection of tea sandwiches on the bottom, traditional English scones in the middle, and decadent pastries on top.

A home-style afternoon tea is more relaxed, with choices varying from Chinese tea to different tea-time snacks based on preferences. Afternoon tea is all about creating a calm and gentle atmosphere, akin to the subtle interactions between ancient Chinese intellectuals. A few glasses of sparkling wine add a bit of cheer, with no pressure or expectation.

My first English afternoon tea was in the mid-1990s. Shortly after starting my PhD in the UK, my supervisor invited our research group to gather at his home. "Just an afternoon tea," he said. At the time, I had been in England for less than three months and felt like an outsider, disoriented and uncertain about the future. However, that first afternoon tea soothed my mind and granted me a brief respite from my homesickness. The conversations had on that day may have faded, but the sense of camaraderie I experienced has been deeply imprinted on my memory.

Since then, I've enjoyed many an afternoon tea. I've had tea in iconic places like the Orchard Tea Garden, a quintessential spot in Cambridge, and tea in more tranquil places, like in a boat along the River Cam. One July afternoon, I even hosted tea for a distinguished professor from Beijing, who was visiting her son at Cambridge. "Afternoon tea? Why?" she asked, puzzled.

"The best option for a poor cook," I smiled.

No kitchen smoke, no bustling restaurants, no boisterous crowds – just a tranquil moment, quietly spent together amid the wild greenery at home. As she quickly came to appreciate, afternoon tea is neither a grand dinner nor a rushed lunch. It is a harmonious interlude where hosts and guests spend time in comfort and at ease.

After nearly thirty years in England, I have come to appreciate the charm of afternoon tea. It is like a mirror of the reserved nature of the British. It can be indoors or outdoors depending on the weather, short or long, rich or simple, with flexible timing. The tea itself might not matter, but who you share it with does. Each person is an individual, and our shared moments can be dazzling or subtle, but each encounter is always unique.

About the author

Xiangyu is a PhD in environmental sciences and an alumnus of the University of Cambridge. Xiangyu has lived in the UK for nearly 30 years and has long been engaged in environmental and climate change research and consultancy.

Foodie in London

Written by: Lin Xue
Translated by: Yurong Li

I blame my mother, a woman born and raised in Sichuan, for turning me into a foodie. And who would have thought that one day, this foodie would find her way to London? Despite its claim to be "the capital of epicures", this metropolis certainly brought me much misery when it comes to food.

Cold dishes and drinks are my biggest source of discomfort. Traditional Chinese medicine holds that the spleen and stomach – the vital organs responsible for generating *qi* and blood – thrive on warm food and drinks. Since ancient times, the Chinese have promoted drinking boiled water, preferably while it's still warm. When visiting friends, the host will always offer a nice cup of hot water the moment a guest enters their home, and for those feeling unwell, a glass of hot water is the first line of defense. However, the British seem unable to live without cold food and drinks.

When I first arrived in the UK, I was warmly welcomed by an elderly couple who kindly treated me to a feast made from whatever they had in their refrigerator. Apart from a few slices of toast struggling to stay lukewarm, the rest of the meal – milk, drinks, cheese, jams and salad – was as chilling as the winter weather. There was hot tea and coffee, but they only came to my rescue after the meal. As for boiled water, it was a distant dream – cold water is evidently a staple in the British diet. Equally cold are the wines and spirits. In traditional Chinese culture, wine is often warmed in a water bath before serving. This warms the stomach, and in winter, the whole body. While people from southern China may not do this as frequently, at the very least, wine is served at room temperature.

The British, however, insist on serving their alcoholic drinks chilled. Ice cubes floating in glasses are a common sight, and every ounce of gin is diluted with tonic water – how odd! It wasn't until later that I learned nearly all "Western alcohol", such as brandy, vodka, whisky, beer, wine and liqueur, is best served chilled, on the rocks or mixed with other beverages to enhance the flavour. The strong alcohol can mask the unique taste of the drink if not balanced this way. But I still can't wrap my head around the idea of serving red wine, with its moderate alcohol content, chilled!

When seeing the British diluting their alcoholic drinks – especially those containing merely 30 to 40 percent of alcohol – some Chinese mistakenly think that the Brits cannot handle their alcohol like the Chinese do. That is simply a misconception. The Brits are fervent followers of Dionysus and not even the inferno itself could stop them from downing a couple more pints, let alone a few more ice cubes and a splash of tonic. The streets of London are teeming with bars, pubs and clubs, always overflowing with cheerful customers. Every night, conversations swell into a roar until customers are reminded it's closing time. If pubs and bars in the UK didn't close by 11 pm, I'm convinced some people would spend not only the entire night but their whole lives there. Thankfully, their need to work during the week to earn a living somewhat curbs their appetite for more pints. Yet, these gentle Dr. Jekylls of the weekday transform swiftly into wasted Mr. Hydes by Friday night.

I had an encounter with one such tipsy creature. I was on a double-decker bus, and when it stopped at a station, a rather chubby fellow tumbled down the stairs. The rumbling and clashing noises heralded his descent. Reeking of alcohol, he struggled to stand on his feet, staggered to the doors, and, as he set foot outside, stumbled again, rolling straight out of the bus and continuing his journey. As the bus drove some distance away, I glanced back and could still spot his hefty figure, now lying completely horizontal on the pavement.

The British also have a sweet tooth. I first noticed this in the yoghurt I used to purchase in the supermarket for 34 pence every day. It was the supermarket's own brand, quite tasty and well-priced. The only problem is the jam it contained – its sweetness could be cloying. Then I discovered that the British never finish a meal without dessert. When I went to visit a family, they were celebrating their teenage son's birthday. The hostess baked a big cake for everyone. It was topped with a little cottage circled with miniature fences and decorated with lawns and flowerbeds, with snow-white icing glowing underneath. Yet this little estate straight out of a fairy tale was built upon a precarious volcano filled with dense chocolate sauce, which oozed out from the edge of the cake like brown lava. It was too sweet – almost criminally so, and I rudely had to leave this beautiful delicacy behind on my plate. Moreover, British sweets are often accompanied by acidity, and many sauces are the union of both – some say that is part of the legacy of the conquering Romans. Lemon is a must in cooking; lemon is to British cuisine what vinegar is to Chinese cuisine.

And don't even get me started on fish and chips – it's far too simplistic to be worthy of a national dish. A fish weighing over 500 grams, barely salted, coated in flour, and deep-fried. Then, it's hastily served with a few pieces of fried potatoes and a small puddle of ketchup – that's it! On that long beach once kissed by Queen Victoria's toes, every restaurant sells fish and chips, and the only thing distinguishing them is the price. Given that the UK is surrounded by oceans, how can fish and chips be the only notable fish dish? Now I understand why fish die with their eyes open – knowing that their fate is to become a stiff, fried morsel, they're unable to close their eyes and die in peace!

It's not that people in the UK hate savoury food; many simply reject it because of health concerns. One day, after the theatre, my friend and I spotted a crowd peering around a doorway – goodness gracious, a Chinese noodle shop! We walked in, filled with excitement and anticipation. But what we were served was a forkful of noodles swimming in plain water with a few drops of soy sauce and a handful of beansprouts as garnish. After thoroughly inspecting it from every angle, I voiced my frustration at such a baffling dish: how can they expect us to swallow this abomination? There wasn't a single drop of oil in sight, let alone the luscious toppings I had been hoping for.

My friend explained that it's because the English believe fatty and oily food isn't good for their health. But that doesn't add up – why do they never reject the butter on their toast? Isn't butter pure fat? At that moment, a wave of homesickness swept over me, and I longed for the noodle bars lining the streets of Chengdu. Their menus, usually written in large characters on a board on the wall, announced blissful bowls of noodles with all sorts of toppings: braised beef, braised ribs, braised pork intestines, minced pork with chilli, pickled pepper with chicken giblets, fried eel with minced garlic, and so much more. Even the famous Dandan noodles come in countless variations, whether topped with crispy fried minced pork or delicate salted pork, and they could be enjoyed with or without broth… every variety is a gourmet dish that no one can refuse.

No matter how sensible and proud they may be, the British can't hold out for long against the temptation of Chinese cuisine, especially that from my hometown, Sichuan. When I was in London many years ago, there were already plenty of Chinese restaurants. The most beloved were the Cantonese places, serving Har Gau and fish porridge, while Sichuan restaurants were also starting to sprout up. Now, London boasts Sichuan-style hotpot chains that have been warmly embraced by the locals. As I write this, I've come across a Londoner's review of Chengdu: Lovely weather, reasonable prices, convenient shopping, excellent public transport, clean streets, and most importantly, amazing food. It was a paradise – if only it weren't for the mosquitoes!

About the author

Lin Xue is a member of Sichuan Writers Association and Chengdu Writers Association. She was a visiting scholar at the Chinese University of Hong Kong (CUHK).

Flower-planting in a Park Sparks Some Thoughts

Written by: Shao Jie
Translated by: Andrew Jin

"Mom, do you want to come plant flowers with me?" My daughter asked.

"Plant flowers? We live in an apartment, there's no garden. Where are we going to plant flowers?" I replied.

It turned out my daughter had signed up for a volunteer activity to plant flowers in a park. This immediately piqued my interest. I am always willing to try new things. Since the pandemic began, I've been travelling back and forth between Shanghai and London. Shanghai is my home, but during the pandemic, the children couldn't go back to Shanghai, so I ended up spending more time in London. Last year, I finally decided to establish a home in London as well. This city is not entirely unfamiliar to me. I came to London in the mid-1990s, got married here, worked and lived here for several years, and then went back to Shanghai. I then returned to London, and back to Shanghai again, repeating this cycle over several years. This familiar yet foreign city always seems to surprise me with something new and different, sparking fresh thoughts.

For instance, this volunteer flower-planting activity.

After registering online, we received a detailed email a few days later, informing us of the date, time and meeting place, along with some precautions and a clearly marked map. It was very user-friendly. I was impressed that for planting flowers, they told us not to bring any tools as they would provide everything. All we needed to bring was a personal water bottle if we didn't want to use their disposable paper cups. Since it was my first time and I didn't know what to expect, I brought two pairs of rubber gloves from home, just in case.

The day arrived quickly. It was already November and at 10am, it was a bit chilly in London. We gathered outside a small cafe at the foot of Primrose Hill. We arrived five minutes early, and a few others joined us gradually. At exactly 10am, a small green maintenance truck labelled "Royal Parks" drove up. A young British woman got out and briefly explained where we would be planting flowers (actually flower seeds) on Primrose Hill. I counted seven of us, including my daughter and me. The truck took the main road while we walked across the lawn to a nearby slope.

At the destination, the British girl introduced the two types of flower seeds we would be planting: Spring Snowflakes and Bluebells. The Spring Snowflake seeds were larger, and she explained that we should dig a hole three to four times the length of the seed. She pointed to some large trees, saying that these flowers liked growing in the shade of trees. By next spring, the flowers we planted would bloom, creating a beautiful scene. Her description immediately conjured up an image of a sea of flowers in my mind. Those familiar with London know that it's a city filled with green spaces and blooming flowers in the spring. This year, I brought my parents to London for a few months. My mother remarked on how many green spaces there were and how freely people could walk on the grass. I jokingly told her, "These are capitalist grasslands; feel free to step on them!"

We started planting, and the tools were indeed handy. I didn't need to use my own rubber gloves. The gloves they provided were much better. There were small shovels, small spades, and a small foam pad to kneel on. Most of the tools were new to me, but once I started using them, they were very effective and in one word: professional! No wonder B&Q (a British DIY and home improvement retailing company) is still thriving here, whereas it has long ceased operations in China. After kneeling and planting for over two hours, my daughter and I had planted about 20 Spring Snowflake seeds and 40 Bluebell seeds. To be honest, it's hard to imagine that such a large park relies on volunteers planting seeds one by one, on their knees. This volunteer activity happens year-round, several times a week, and all you need to do is register online to join – it's very simple. While planting, we encountered several earthworms. Sometimes we accidentally cut them in half, which made us feel sorry. The soil two inches below the surface was moist and loose, but deeper down it was dry and hard. It was quite tiring, and my back and hands were sore.

Midway through the two-hour activity, we had a 15-minute coffee break, gathering by the truck to drink coffee and eat cookies brought by the British girl. She asked each of us about our jobs and what we usually do. British people are always reserved, and no one dominates the conversation. Everyone spoke briefly, softly and gently about where they were from and what they did. There is always a sense of restraint in the initial conversation between strangers in Britain. No one makes loud jokes, and everyone is careful not to say too much, yet they do not make you feel too distant. This sense of propriety is something I haven't seen in other cultures. Among the seven of us, two were PhD holders. The British girl had just finished her PhD and worked in a lab for a few years but decided that wasn't the life she wanted, so she quit and joined Royal Parks to work in park maintenance (to Chinese people, this might seem like a waste – why would a PhD holder leave a lab job to dig in a park? But she was at peace with it, doing what she liked). Another volunteer had a PhD in psychology, and there was a retired teacher and an older-looking software engineer who was still working. Apart from my daughter and me, there was another Chinese girl who was the loudest among us. She laughed heartily and spoke loudly. A straightforward person from Shandong, she said she wanted to be a gardener, but jobs were hard to find, so she started with volunteer activities.

The 2.5-hour volunteer activity ended quickly. The next day, the British girl sent the first email, thanking us for our selfless contribution.

I carefully read the email and was touched not only by the photos she sent of us planting but also by the links to detailed information about the two types of flowers we planted. Clicking on the links, I could read about various aspects of these flowers, how to care for them, suitable seasons, soil types, and their classification. This attention to detail made me feel that this was not just a flower-planting experience, but that the organisers took the volunteer work seriously and professionally. The care that she showed to thank us for our time and effort was quite moving.

A few days later, the British girl sent another email, inviting past volunteers to join another hedgerow planting activity.

After participating in this volunteer activity, I had some thoughts. In Shanghai, arguably the best-managed city in China in terms of greenery and cleanliness, the city's beauty relies on countless gardeners and cleaners. It has little to do with the ordinary residents living there. In Shanghai, I also participate in some volunteer activities, like those organised by social welfare groups, but the willingness and persistence of volunteers seems to depend more on their passion. Public welfare organisations seem limited in what they can do, often lacking two things: resources and money. But how many participants (volunteers) have money or resources? Many volunteers of the gardening activity joined because it was a nice day, or the park was in a convenient location for them, or because they love flowers – volunteering their time was not a burden. In China, however, volunteers often need great enthusiasm and persistence to accomplish something, which is not easy. A good friend once told me that if doing public welfare doesn't make you happy, you shouldn't do it. Yet, in reality, many people in China persist in volunteering, even when unhappy. They impose on themselves the need to be loving, persistent and dedicated to society. I'm not saying this is bad, it's just that the values in the two countries are so different. In China, we emphasise sacrifice, especially a silent sacrifice, as a noble virtue. Why can't Chinese people do things more easily, without making every task seem profound, laborious and painstaking?

From another perspective, public welfare organisations should focus on making it easy and enjoyable for volunteers to participate in activities. The feeling of being taken seriously in a volunteer activity is far more important than just relying on the dedication of volunteers. Achieving sustainability, mutual respect, and no sense of indebtedness on either side is the essence of volunteering, in my opinion. How can this be achieved? This gardening volunteer activity and the subsequent emails from Royal Parks provided an excellent model. Any volunteer activity should provide value to potential volunteers. If a volunteer activity allows you to learn something or enrich yourself in some way, you won't feel the need for tearful persistence. You can participate and learn in various ways, and it's okay if you eventually stop participating.

In London, our daily life in the community – libraries, hospitals, museums and other public places – provides numerous opportunities for ordinary residents to participate in the community and the city's construction. Sometimes I wonder, what exactly is "home"? I've lived in Shanghai for 20 years and still feel it is unfamiliar. I've lived in London for nearly eight years, and I feel that as long as I'm willing, I can understand this city from every corner. Of course, I can actively try to understand Shanghai, and I believe there are plenty of opportunities to get involved in civic activities if I put in the time and effort. However, somehow, this seems much easier to do in London. Perhaps civilisation, to some extent, is about creating a platform for ordinary people to participate and engage without burden.

I eagerly await next spring so that I can return to Primrose Hill and proudly say, "Look, those are snowflakes, and those are bluebells – such lovely names for such lovely flowers, planted by me!"

About the author

Shao Jie is currently retired. She used to work in the British Council Shanghai and London offices, promoting British culture and education. In her spare time, she likes painting, writing and reading books; She is also an active traveller and she has travelled around seven continents. She came to London in the mid-1990s and has lived and worked in Shanghai and London with her husband and two children for the past 30 years.

Land of Gardens

Written by: Zou Wanqiao
Translated by: Laura Giulia Bonsaver

Garden flowers are ubiquitous in the UK. Everywhere you look, you will see a bright burst of colours. Even window ledges are filled with flowers in bloom. It seems that no single flower claims the season's crown, and seasons are not defined by one colour, but by hundreds. Flowers blossom all around you: the ever-changing fuchsias, the sublime wild rose mallows, the elegant irises, the sprightly spider flowers… Coming here brings back memories from my long-bygone childhood, and of a time when my mother brought home the DVD of her favourite cartoon from her own childhood, *Floral Fairies*. Each night before bed, she would put on an episode for us to watch. As a small child, I was naturally curious, and I eagerly engaged with the programme, waving at each of the floral fairies.

Around 2014 when I first landed in London, I marvelled at the stunning display of flowers everywhere. Filled with curiosity, I opened my map and spotted a gigantic park. To my surprise, it was not Disneyland or any kind of amusement park; it was simply a park named Kew Gardens. And so, I went. Arriving in this beautiful garden, I was struck by the vibrant colours of the season's hydrangeas. Somehow, the roses looked so different from any I'd seen in flower shops. I walked along the Treetop Walkway where visitors can stroll past the uppermost branches of the giant sequoias, and only children dare to skip freely along the path at such heights. Before coming to London, I hadn't heard anything about this wonderful park.

While living in London later as a graduate student, whenever a flower-themed exhibition took place at Kew Gardens or new flowers came into bloom, I'd be back there in a flash.

The first time I visited Kew Gardens, it was during the Black Friday Christmas light show, and I had a close brush with danger. While my friends stayed back on Oxford Street, I decided to head out early with another classmate. On the bus, a fellow Asian passenger struck up a conversation and, upon hearing my destination, widened his eyes in disbelief. "So late and so far?" he said.

As I waited in the garden café next to Kew Gardens, I checked my social media and saw that chaos had erupted on Oxford Street shortly after I left. Apparently, someone had yelled "run", and everyone started to panic, thinking it was a life-threatening situation. People believed they were facing a disaster, only to later find out it was a false alarm.

This incident underscored the constant worry that follows us in a foreign land, where every day can bring unforeseen challenges.

Later, during the Christmas season, I had another surprise – this one a bit more amusing. I didn't expect mistletoe to leave such an impression on me. In Kew Gardens, these mysterious flowers had been arranged into beautiful bouquets and hung upside down all around the site. At first, I thought the staff had hung the flowers to dry, just like they do in our tea houses at home, and I assumed that these flowery decorations were simply there for tourists to take photos. But later, I realised this was not the case.

Before I came to the UK, I thought Christmas was just like our Lunar New Year, a holiday reserved solely for family gatherings. But looking around at the mistletoe hanging in dimly lit restaurants filled with young couples, I couldn't help but wonder why the atmosphere felt so romantic. It felt so different from anything I had seen in films and on TV. I started to feel a little embarrassed around mistletoe and would move awkwardly away from it if I came across it with my classmates. Back at home, Qixi Festival, a national festival that originally did not have romantic connotations, has evolved into Chinese Lovers' Day. Had this happened to Christmas too? I discovered later that this wasn't the case at all. It turns out there is a custom of kissing under the mistletoe, something I only discovered by chance while watching *The Ancient Magus' Bride* anime.

Standing at the ticket entrance of Kew Gardens, I met a young American man who spoke Chinese and was interning at the gardens. Eager to practise his Mandarin, we chatted for a bit. I felt envious of him for having the chance to work at Kew Gardens. Looking a little fed up, he said wryly, "Well, maybe if you saw all the sweeping and pruning that I have to do, you wouldn't be so envious!"

In the spring, I attended an orchid exhibition. I thought there would be no better place to see orchids than in China, since we have adored these flowers for thousands of years. But I never dreamt that elegant white orchids with such long, flowing petals could be grown in England. Through the misty steam of the Kew Garden greenhouse, they reminded me of Xiaolongnü, a character from a Chinese novel. It looked as if her figure, as white as snow, was emerging from the depths of the pool. That day, I happened to attend a talk on "Seed Banks" led by a British PhD student who had recently graduated from Chiang Mai University. She spoke about various methods of seed preservation, especially for seeds grown in tropical climates that can easily rot. She also discussed certain plants that appear nearly identical yet possess entirely distinct DNA. It's funny. Despite having no trace of botanical expertise on my CV, I still vividly recall much of what I learnt. Deep down, I truly admired this young woman. She travelled thousands of miles in pursuit of her passion; to study the subject she loves at a university unknown to most. To her, it did not matter that the subject might seem obscure to many people. She followed her heart and ultimately found her place.

In April, I brought along two of my friends to see the azalea exhibition. On arrival, we saw a couple of staff members giving a lecture. They were very professional. It felt as though we were sitting in a university lecture. Walking through the exhibition afterwards, we were captivated by the brilliant colours of a watercolour painting. A local lady took an interest in me and asked if I was studying horticulture. That day, I happened to be wearing a dark blue floral dress. Perhaps it was this dress that had caught the attention of the lady, a fellow flower lover. We began chatting. At some point in the conversation, she mentioned wisteria being from Japan, but I quickly corrected her. Japan imported many plants from China in the past. She returned with a question, asking if China had yellow wisteria. Indeed, I had never seen yellow wisteria in China, and come to think of it, I had seen more colours of wisteria in Japanese travel advertisements…but that didn't necessarily mean wisteria originated in Japan, right? Changing the subject, I told her that I was surprised not to see any peonies in Kew Gardens, considering its incredibly diverse collection of flowers. Keen to show us that the gardens did have peonies, the lady led us to a secluded flowerbed with some single-petal varieties in bloom. Later, my classmate insisted that she was "pretty sure those weren't peonies." At that time, I wasn't very knowledgeable myself about peony varieties, so I let it drop.

It wasn't until 2023, when I happened to win a book titled *The Plant Collectors* through a competition on the social media app Weibo, that I discovered the many fascinating tales behind the plants in this garden. I learnt that it is thanks to the adventurous plant hunters that Kew Gardens possesses such a vibrant array of flowers from around the world. Interestingly, some of the flowers that plant hunters brought home were not necessarily collected from their native habitats. The plant hunters may have found the seeds in a particular place, but those seeds might have already travelled across multiple countries or continents.

The newly restored glass palace at Kew was unveiled just in time for the azalea exhibition. It had been under renovation for years, and we had waited so long to see it. When I had first visited the gardens, it had been closed to the public. Now, nearly six years later, I was able to see it. Like a good "Floral Fairy", I plan to return to Kew for many years to come.

About the author

Zou Wanqiao has a master's in Accounting and Finance from the University of Southampton and is a member of both the Tianjin Poetry Society and the Nankai University Poetry and Couplet Society. Wanqiao has published more than 30 poems in journals such as *Poetry Monthly* and *Poetry Newspaper* and is the author of *Translation and Annotation of Tanghu Xunpu.*

England to Me

Written by: Gu Yu
Translated by: Tong Pan

Anyone who has travelled extensively is likely to have their own unique narrative. In this distinctive story, you might assume the role of the protagonist, with the ground beneath your feet and the place names in your memory serving as crucial elements. I have just edited the Chinese version of *England to Me* by Emily Hahn. Thus, inspired by this great work, I shall tell my own story.

When I was 20, I didn't understand or enjoy my English and American Literature course in university because the lecturer, who had a PhD degree, used a lot of jargon. I can only recall how "Araby", a short story by James Joyce, filled the air with dullness. Fortunately, at this time, a lovely young guy entered my life for the first time. He was enrolled in a Sino-British joint education programme and, as planned, advanced to the British partner institution. Shortly after, he chose to end our relationship without any explanation. Since then, a seed was sown in my heart to "study in the UK". For a long time, the unnamed youngster in "Araby", tortured by his studies and eager to go to the market, lingered in my thoughts. I tried to console him with the phrase, "Good things come to those who wait."

It was after this that I discovered James Joyce was not English, as I had assumed, but Irish, and that his early experiences had a profound influence on his writing. As I delved deeper into psychology and education, I learned about the "Zeigarnik effect", and eventually, I found myself standing on the platform, lecturing as a professor. No matter how much I read, my favourite short story remained "Araby".

Faced with many cohorts of students, I consistently performed three key tasks. First, I guided students through an analysis of the boy's character, encouraging them to consider what kind of person would choose a book solely based on its colour. Secondly, I shared the writer Ge Fei's commentary on the story and invited students to connect it to their own life experiences. Lastly, I urged students to pick up their brushes and sketch images inspired by the most striking section of the text.

Rather than me simply teaching them how to read attentively, it often felt more like a group of young friends helping me create a shared sanctuary through literature.

My true understanding of England beyond literature began eight years ago when I met an English instructor named J. A colleague had warned me that working with foreign instructors could be challenging, not to mention the cultural differences and certain peculiar temperaments of some foreigners.

But how could I resist the allure of "Araby"? Against the odds, J and I, both new instructors fresh out of school, decided to give it a try. Surprisingly, this challenge led to a close friendship. J was honest and dedicated to teaching. One year, the whole school voted him "The Most Popular Teacher". Although his degree was in physics, he had a deep interest in language and literature, and I often sought his advice on these subjects. His guidance has been invaluable to all my translation projects so far. He was like my British Doraemon, with exceptional translation skills and a talent for explaining cultural differences. Of course, I also helped him a great deal. I purchased numerous primary school Chinese textbooks and organised volunteers to teach him Chinese, laying the foundation for his future studies.

J also experienced a significant event at our school. A fire broke out in a garage just beneath our office building. Fortunately, there were no casualties. While my Chinese colleagues and I assumed it was simply bad luck and trusted the school to handle the situation, J and another British teacher demanded a thorough explanation. As a result, a meeting was held between the foreign instructors and several school administrators to address the issue. Naturally, as J's collaborating teacher, I took on the role of interpreter. After quickly familiarising myself with basic fire-related vocabulary, I attended the meeting, which covered the school's recent fire safety procedures. J expressed his satisfaction after reviewing all the information. It was as if the school leaders were hosting a real press conference!

At first, I was puzzled by J's reaction, as he wasn't even in the office when the fire occurred. But as I gained more experience, I came to understand him fully. During IELTS (an English proficiency test for non-native English speakers) invigilation, I grew accustomed to giving clear instructions on where candidates should evacuate. Every time I visited the British Library, I noticed that not only did the reading rooms have ordinary carrels, but there were also special small rooms for disabled readers. And each time I finished shopping at the supermarket, the cashier and the customer behind me would patiently wait for me to pack all my items before serving the next customer...

The arrival of English instructor A introduced me to new Sino-British friendships. Unlike J, A had a humanities background and was about 12 years my senior. But these differences didn't matter. In reality, A was well-versed in various computer applications and mobile apps, and she had a knack for winning people over.

Due to work commitments, A and I were required to co-host an online English summer course in August, which was scheduled to run for a month. Initially, I wasn't sure if I'd get along with her as well as I did with J. To my surprise, A was highly dedicated, even offering to teach language and culture classes to students in the morning, China time, despite the inconvenience it caused her in the UK. We ended our collaboration on a cheerful note, having made a good impression on the students.

Shortly before the new term began, A arrived in China and quickly became a favourite on campus. Wherever she went, she greeted people warmly and naturally, and many international students were drawn to her, often approaching her for a chat. Who says the British are reserved? Who says they only like to talk about the weather? A had been teaching in the UK for nearly 20 years and had educated a large number of Chinese students, many of whom had gone on to earn master's and doctoral degrees. However, this was her first visit to the homeland of her former students, and she couldn't hide her excitement.

I could hardly contain my happiness when, three years ago, I finally realised my dream of studying in the UK. I often think back on the enjoyable and exhilarating time I spent as a visiting scholar at the University of Cambridge. My joy stemmed from the inspiring words of the poet Xu Zhimo, while the adventure came from navigating the many challenges posed by the pandemic. When facing new challenges, I sometimes quietly ask myself if they are as difficult as my experiences during the pandemic in the UK.

Fortunately, I changed jobs this year to work at a Sino-foreign cooperative education institution, which partners with a school in the UK. My workplace embraced my idea for a decorative design, and every time I enter my office, I pass by a crimson couch and a picture of willow leaves on the wall. The vibrancy of the couch reminds me of the cosy embrace of the lazy seat beside the floor-to-ceiling windows in the English Department Library at Cambridge, while the graceful pattern of the willow leaves evokes the sense of optimism William Morris hoped to inspire in future generations. I hope my students will appreciate them as much as I do.

Youth may fade, wrinkles will appear, and not all global issues will have clear solutions. Yet, what matters most is that I can say the river of my life carries with it waves from England. These waves carry Peter Rabbit's sweat and tears from his adventures in the vegetable garden; they once dove into the River Cam to play with the punts; and now they flow into the Thames, quietly watching Tower Bridge open and close. Thanks to these wonderful, if not always fearsome, tales of England, my horizons have been broadened.

About the author

Gu Yu is an English instructor with PhD in Literature. The author of *The Anxiety of the Guardian: A Study on the Growth Patterns in Pearl Buck's Works*, and the first translator of *Stories and Poems for Smart Kids*.

Buying Books: Rediscovering Trust in the UK

Written by: Li Xinsheng
Translated by: Wang Hanyu and Xinyao

British people have a profound love for buying and reading books. The book market is an indispensable part of every Briton's life, which is why the UK's per capita book ownership, reading volume and number of bookstores are among the highest in the world.

Almost every British town boasts its own historic bookshop. Many Britons living in small towns cherish the serene charm of the countryside, finding it far from mundane or repetitive. These towns are well-connected by transport, self-sufficient, and still bustling with life. The story behind the rise of the small town of Hay-on-Wye would seem almost unimaginable to many in China. In recent years, the UK has witnessed a "reverse migration" of bookshops, exemplified by establishments like the Francis Edwards antiquarian bookshop, once thriving in London's West End before finding a new home in this charming small town. Moreover, large cities and university towns such as London, Edinburgh, Cambridge and Oxford are home to countless bookshops that serve not only as retail outlets for new books and textbooks but also as havens for rare and second-hand literary treasures. These bookshops cater not just to the general public but also fulfill crucial roles in library acquisitions and government subscriptions.

Having spent nearly half a year in the UK, I've had the opportunity to explore second-hand bookshops not only in London, Cambridge and Oxford but also further afield in Hay-on-Wye, known as the "Kingdom of Antique Books". My journey has also led me through a variety of book markets, including the Market Square Book Market and the Book Sale at St Botolph's Church – both in Cambridge – and the South Bank Book Market in London. In addition, I've enjoyed attending the regular antiquarian book fairs organised by the Provincial Booksellers Fairs Association (PBFA).

When I visited the London Autumn Book Fair, for instance, the fair was bustling with activity, yet there were only a handful of Chinese attendees and young people. As I lingered by the stall of a British bookseller, he warmly remarked, "Don't be put off by the prices on the books. If you're interested, we can always negotiate."

After the fair, I searched online for some books that caught my eye, such as *The Flowers of Shakespeare* and *The Classes and Orders of the Linnaean System of Botany*, but found no sellers from the UK. This shows that many British bookshops have not entered the international market through second-hand trading platforms. A prime example is the well-known Cambridge bookshop, G. David Bookseller. It firmly refuses to open an online store. The owners claim that this is to maintain direct contact with customers and preserve the joy of discovery for readers.

This kind of old-fashioned approach is not uncommon in the UK. Plurabelle Books in Cambridge, the shop I visit the most frequently, is another example. Due to the sheer volume of their collection, many books are unpriced, leaving ample room for on-the-spot bargaining. The shop also houses a considerable number of non-English books that the owner often has no idea how to price, frequently asking me for advice on their value.

I have found numerous hidden gems from Plurabelle Books, including Chinese books from the collection of Professor David McMullen, a renowned Sinologist, mentor to the famous author Jin Yong, and a lifetime fellow at St. John's College, Cambridge, and Director of the Chinese Studies Centre. Among the finds were also illustrated books from the Meiji period.

The bookstore operates solely through its physical store and its own online shop. In the shop description, they clearly state:

> "We cannot compete with mega sellers who pretend to be charities, sell books for pennies and in the process destroy the marketplace for second-hand books. We will not compete with information brokerage like digital copies and print on demand. But we continue to give you a serious and dedicated service which is focused on the individuality of each single book: its condition, its origin, sometimes even its smell. You come to us for real books, not just instances of ISBNs."

Despite my appreciation for this type of service, I simply don't have the time or energy to visit all the major second-hand bookstores across the UK. For the most part, I have to rely on large second-hand book trading platforms to guide me in my search, such as my longtime favourite, Mike Park Books. It was through a bookseller's suggestion that I began selecting books from their website and establishing direct contact for purchases.

Compared to private websites run by individual sellers, international second-hand book trading platforms typically charge higher fees of often around 10% to 15% of the book's price. In such cases, opting for private transactions directly with sellers can create a win-win situation. The platforms are generally open and accommodating in this regard, and bypassing the platform is tacitly accepted. That said, not everyone is comfortable with private transactions due to the inherent risks.

The first time I contacted a seller directly, I discovered that a book priced over a hundred pounds could be bought with a 10% discount if purchased directly from the seller, which was very tempting. There are typically five methods for private transactions: direct bank transfer, PayPal, receiving a payment invoice from the seller, placing an order on the seller's private website, and in-person transactions. The first method is the most commonly used, while in-person transactions can sometimes yield even greater discounts.

Initially, I was hesitant about a direct bank transfer and sought advice from several Chinese individuals who had lived and worked in the UK for years. One tutor admitted he had never tried this method and refrained from commenting on it. A postdoctoral researcher advised caution, as bad people exist everywhere. However, a driver with over two decades of experience in the UK thought it was no big deal, as he believed that British people are inclined to avoid trouble and wouldn't risk conflict over a small amount of money.

Ultimately, lured by the potential of a bargain, I made the payment and, with some anxiety, waited a few days. To my relief, the book arrived as promised. The seller had been trustworthy and turned me into a compulsive online second-hand book shopper.

In total, I did more than twenty private transactions, with amounts ranging from £50 to £2,000, and I have purchased books from as far away as the Netherlands and Germany. To be honest, if I were defrauded within the UK, I might still have a chance to visit the seller in person to resolve the issue. For the European sellers, without a Schengen visa and unwilling to spend a fortune on a trip to Europe, if the books didn't arrive, I would have to accept it and consider it a charitable donation. Yet, without exception so far, I have received all the books.

That's not to say I have never been worried. For my largest purchase, three volumes of *Curtis's Botanical Magazine* costing over £2,000, I felt particularly anxious. After paying on Thursday, I sent follow-up emails on Friday and Saturday, but received no response. I was on the verge of contacting the police but was concerned that my broken English would make it difficult for me to explain the situation clearly. Visiting the seller was also out of the question, as the address provided was too vague and imprecise to locate. This left me in a state of distress. Then, on Sunday, I suddenly received an email from the seller explaining the delay: the owner was away on a business trip, and the wife of the owner was on crutches. Thus, the bookseller had only just managed to respond. Reading this, I breathed a sigh of relief.

Later, I spoke with Mr. Wang, a tutor and fellow enthusiast of Western antiquarian books. He reassured me that there was absolutely no need to worry. Although based in China, he had purchased books from all over the world, placing hundreds of orders without ever being scammed. He believed that international booksellers were highly reputable. His only close call was with an Australian bookseller who was rather slow in dispatching the order. After waiting for over a week, Mr. Wang mustered the courage to send an email, expressing that this had been his worst global shopping experience. The bookseller immediately arranged for shipment, sincerely apologised, and explained that he had been overwhelmed with work.

Isn't this how people should interact? Keeping promises and acting with integrity. Trust should be established not only among acquaintances but also strangers. Of course, this is not to say that there are no swindlers in the

UK, but the honest practices of British booksellers have greatly enhanced my impression of the British people. Perhaps this integrity is one reason why British bookstores, many of which have been around for fifty or even a hundred years, continue to thrive. Running a bookstore has thus become a highly respected profession. British bookstores represent far more than a means of making money; they embody a sense of social responsibility. The decades, even centuries, of reputation and influence that a bookstore cultivates are preserved and passed down. Therefore, it is difficult for British booksellers to fall into moral disrepute.

Richard Booth, the "King of Hay-on-Wye", dedicated his life to the development of this small town, ultimately transforming it into a global destination for book lovers. The town is also home to the Hay Festival, a well-known literary festival that attracts celebrities, philanthropists and volunteers. Yuean Fu, a senior editor from Taiwan once said, "A bookstore is inherently a service industry with the mission of cultural dissemination. If you lack social awareness, you should pursue another line of work."

I am also reminded of a conversation from *Nicholas Barker on Book Collecting* (*Shanghai Review of Books*, 2 August 2020). The interviewer asked, "In recent years, the prices of artworks have soared. One reason is that they have become part of the investment portfolios of the wealthy. Many buyers don't necessarily love art, but they buy pieces and then store them in bank vaults without ever looking at them. Do you think there is a similar trend in the investment of rare books?"

Barker candidly replied, "Thank God, this is extremely rare in book collecting. Book collectors are, first and foremost, book lovers. Few people collect books purely for investment. If someone hopes to get rich from book collecting, they've chosen the wrong way to make money; they should pursue something else."

This sentiment echoes the reality that running a bookstore is not a path to wealth. In fact, whether in the East or the West, opening a bookstore has never been a shortcut to riches. While it can provide a livelihood, it's seldom a lucrative venture. This explains why most bookstore owners and attendees at large book fairs in the UK are elderly. Young people, both financially and temperamentally, are unlikely to see running a bookstore as a solid career choice. The typical owner of a bookstore I encountered was often an elderly individual deeply immersed in literature. British booksellers, in particular, are usually well-educated and active in community service, often playing the role of local community leaders.

For instance, George Marrin, the owner of Marrin's Bookshop, is a true expert on local history. He and his wife Doris, a teacher, are cherished members of their community. Every time George discovers a rare gem, he is filled with excitement, often saying to his son during auctions or valuations, "This is better than work, isn't it?"

About the author

Li Xinsheng, Associate Professor in the Department of History at the School of Humanities, Southeast University in China; Director of the Center for the History of Science and Technology at Southeast University; Member of The Writers Association of Jiangsu Province; Member of the China Science Writers Association.

Collecting Second-hand Goods in the UK

Written by: Chen Zhihao
Translated by: Yukun Peng

When you think of the UK, what comes to mind? Is it the ancient castles and stately homes, the magnificent royal palaces, or perhaps the great literary figures like Shakespeare and Dickens? Maybe it's the infamous weather or the well-known dish: fish and chips? For me, after nine years in the UK, I've developed a fascination for collecting various second-hand goods from charity shops.

Charity shops are a unique and charming aspect of British communities. Whether in bustling cities or quaint villages, you'll find them lining the high streets. These shops not only serve a charitable purpose but also embody community spirit and environmental consciousness. Typically run by charitable organizations, they sell donated second-hand items such as clothes, books, furniture, electronics, toys and more. Common charity shops include Oxfam, the British Heart Foundation, Cancer Research UK, Traid, which focuses on improving the textile industry and reducing clothing waste, and Age UK, which supports the elderly, among many others.

From my observations, these shops are usually small but very well-organised. Clothes and shoes are neatly sorted by style, colour and season, making it rare to find two identical pieces of clothing in the same shop, as everything is donated by local residents. Shopping in a second-hand store feels a bit like opening a mystery box – you never know what treasures await. Personally, I enjoy buying various second-hand plates and hunting for interesting little items in these shops. However, the quality of goods can vary depending on the area and a bit of luck.

I also love exploring the British countryside, where delightful surprises can often be found in the most unexpected corners. After finishing my master's thesis in 2017, I joined a local Chinese tour group for a three-day trip to the Scottish Highlands. Listening to the chatty tourists felt like being back in China. During a stop in the small town of Pitlochry, I wandered into a charity shop and was immediately drawn to a beautiful porcelain plate hidden in the corner. It had intricate patterns and designs that seemed to whisper stories from a bygone era.

As I squatted to examine it closely, an elderly lady with a Scottish accent approached me. "It's a lovely day today, isn't it? Interested in that plate?" she asked, smiling. I replied, "Yes, I'm quite taken by these plates. They seem to be at least fifty or sixty years old." The lady smiled and said, "These are indeed special, from the early 20th century. They belonged to an old gentleman from the area who passed away, and his family donated his belongings to our shop."

Hearing this story made me even more captivated by the plates. They were priced modestly at £5. I decided to buy one, not just for its beauty but also for its history and the stories it carried, making it truly unique. For me, it was like owning a small luxury item. A fellow Chinese tourist, initially dismissive of second-hand goods, found a lovely tea set in the same shop and was thrilled. This kind of experience has happened to me many times. Over the years, I've visited at least a hundred charity shops across the UK, collecting everything from tableware, small appliances and books to records and trinkets. The shopping process always brings a sense of warmth and goodwill from these shops.

You might think, with such a variety of old clothes and shoes at such low prices, only people from low-income backgrounds shop there. But you'd be mistaken. Charity shop customers are very diverse. Many local British influencers shop in these stores and share tips on styling. Fashion is often a cycle, and many young people and university students shop in these stores to embrace the vintage trend.

Some might wonder how the habit of shopping for second-hand goods became so ingrained in British households. The UK has a long history of charity work, and the development of charity shops dates back to the 19th century. They originated from the initiatives of charitable organisations that sought to raise funds for their causes and provide employment opportunities for disadvantaged groups. During the early to mid-20th century, the two World Wars made charity shops increasingly important. They supplied much-needed goods to war-affected areas. During World War II, with clothing rationed, charity shops became essential sources of clothing. The modern concept of Oxfam's charity shops began after World War II, in 1947, with the opening of their first store in Oxford to aid Greece's post-war recovery. Following a call for donations, people from all over contributed, and part of the profits from the sold goods went to Greece.

Since then, the number of second-hand retail stores has grown. According to recent statistics, there are approximately 11,250 charity shops across the UK. They raise about £270 million annually to support causes like poverty alleviation, medical research, improving the lives of underprivileged children, and enhancing the quality of life for the elderly. These shops employ around 26,800 people and have 186,800 volunteers, including retirees and young people.

Charity shops have created a sustainable business model that balances people, the environment, and profits. For many elderly volunteers, especially those living alone, working in these shops significantly improves their mental health, helping them combat loneliness and fostering a sense of community involvement and achievement. If you ever visit the UK, make sure to explore the local charity shops.

About the author

Chen Zhihao is an Assistant Professor of Business Management at Oxford Brookes University. His research focuses on the spatial behaviours of tourists and the mining of big data in tourism.

Afterword

The Vitality of Everyday Life and Cultural Roots

Written by: Xuemo
Translated by: Kaidi Lyu

My lifelong mission has been to serve as a bridge of literature and culture, and I hope that through my writings, I can connect Chinese literature and traditional culture to the world, and how fortunate it is that this bridge does not stand alone. When attending the London Book Fair, I met yet another bridge – Xinran's Mothers' Bridge of Love and its volunteers. The shared cultural aspiration between us has persuaded me to show great joys and support when the book *HaHa! Britain* was taking its shape, and later when Xinran asked me to furnish it with an epilogue, I was more than happy to oblige.

Though my time in Britain was brief, just a few days at The London Book Fair during which I felt like a fleeting visitor, I formed a unique connection with this place, a connection bridged by none other than Shakespeare.

I have great respect for Tolstoy, but I disagree with him on Shakespeare. Tolstoy condemned the plays of Shakespeare as overly pretentious. I understand his criticism – Tolstoy's straightforward writing style and lofty spirit meant he naturally couldn't appreciate the exaggerated expressions of Shakespeare. However, plays are dramas after all, and dramas are expected to be dramatic. And in pursuit of drama, exaggeration is inevitable. As for that pretentious air, one cannot blame Shakespeare alone – the only "crime" he committed was being British, and thus inheriting that distinctive national trait of being a bit hoity-toity. And let's face it, that touch of pretentiousness is part of British charm: whether in solemnity or in levity, there's always an underlying hint of superiority.

Yet Shakespeare is like the gooey and mellow filling in a custard cream, sandwiched by hard criticism. On one side is Tolstoy, who dislikes his pretentiousness. And on the other side are British aristocrats who disliked him for not being pretentious enough. Even though that earthy, folkloric and Shakespearean simplicity could elicit hearty laughter from Queen Elizabeth I herself, the aristocrats still despised his plays, as their folkish characteristics were, in their eyes, signs of low social standing and vulgarity.

I, however, adore these earthy flavours. How could a tree – whether it be literature or culture – thrive if its roots are not deeply embedded in the soil of everyday life? This book is a collection of vibrant and lively accounts, and the source of their vitality lies in daily life itself. Every Chinese person who sets foot on the British Isles first faces the challenge of navigating everyday life. Those loftier ambitions, like spreading culture, come only after this hurdle is crossed.

During my short stay in London for the Book Fair, I found myself primarily grappling with the intricacies of life here. I took a keen interest in the locals – observing their daily routines, preferences, literary tastes and habits.

It is everyday life that readers of my books are first introduced to. For instance, the *Desert Trilogy* depicts rural life in western China during the 1980s. Similarly, when we delve into the works of Shakespeare or Tolstoy, the journey begins with life itself before progressing to deeper reflections on humanity and culture. This is why I hold Tolstoy and Shakespeare in such high regard.

Before touring the West with my books, I had always assumed that most overseas Chinese still served as vessels of Chinese civilisation, with a beating Chinese heart and a deep love for their culture. However, I found that this wasn't always the case. While some do indeed hold fast to their cultural roots, many more are gradually becoming part of foreign soil.

Take Chinese Americans, for example. When I visited Washington, I attended several gatherings and ceremonies with Chinese people from across the United States. Chinese elites from various fields seemed eager to shed their Chinese identity. They repeatedly emphasised their American citizenship, professed their love for the United States, highlighted the amount of tax they had paid, and underscored their contributions to the prosperity of the US. And there I was, listening to their speeches in shock.

Yet, shock aside, when I placed myself in their shoes, I felt sorrow and bitterness. How hard they had laboured to integrate themselves into American culture and gain a ticket to the elite club! And yet I knew, deep down, that this was impossible. They are destined to become lost, and, worse still, to face despair.

I've also met Chinese living abroad in peace and confidence. And they all share one virtue: to maintain their cultural roots. And surprisingly, they were not discriminated against, but rewarded with respect.

When talking about the founding principles of western nations and China, we cannot assert which is right and which is wrong, as their goals are different, if not opposing from time to time. However, communication and dialogue between the two are essential. And the universal language that can achieve such a dialogue is wisdom and love.

Lastly, I would like to express my deep gratitude to the "Mothers' Bridge of Love" for their efforts in fostering cultural exchanges between the East and the West. "Motherly love" isn't just found in breathing beings; it dwells in all things in the universe and manifests as a profound spiritual principle. The Chinese traditional culture we aim to spread embraces this very spirit: nurturing all things without possessing them, helping others without seeking credit, shaping and benefiting all beings without controlling them. May this "motherly love" reach every corner of the world.

About the author

Xuemo is a distinguished Chinese writer, Vice Chairman of the Gansu Writers Association, and Director of the Guangzhou Institute of Shangpa Culture. His works, including *Desert Rites*, *Hunter's Plains*, and *White Tiger Pass* have been included in research projects in multiple high education institutions such as Peking University, Fudan University, Lanzhou University and Minzu University of China.

Acknowledgments

As the founder of The Mothers' Bridge of Love (MBL), I sincerely thank the following individuals and organisations for their invaluable contributions and selfless support in the creation of this book.

I extend my heartfelt gratitude to all the authors (listed alphabetically by surname), who are also volunteers of MBL: Cai Fang, Cao Tingting, Chen Yan, Chen Zhihao, Ding Xuan, Du Yubin, Fan Xuequn, Gu Hongyan, Gu Yu, He Kai, He Yue, Ji Yang, Li Xinsheng, Lin Xue, Liu Qian, Qu Leilei, Shao Jie, Song Guming, Sun Hong, Sun Lin, Tian Tian, Aurora Wang, Wang Li, Wen Diya, Wu Fan, Xiao Chunduan, Xiaohei, Xiangyu, Xuemo, Yao Feiyan, Yiwen, Yu Shan, Zhang Heruijie, Zhang Ye, Zhang Yidong, Rebekah Zhao, Zhai Maona, Zhe'an, Zimin and Zou Wanqiao.

The stories and personal experiences they have shared from across the British Isles will be preserved for future generations, serving as a model of mutual understanding and trust among diverse cultures.

Heartfelt thanks to the editorial teams of MBL and River Cam Breeze. If this book is destined to become a new milestone in the history of Sino-British cultural exchange, these two teams are the unseen hands that have quietly and diligently raised this monument.

Special thanks to the artists who contributed their work: Feng Tang, who provided the original artwork of Big Ben for the cover; Qu Leilei, the calligrapher of the book title; and Tian Tian, who created the cover design and the illustrations throughout the book. Their original creations have brought vibrant vitality to this work.

Gratitude is also extended to all the volunteering translators (listed alphabetically by surname): Laura Giulia Bonsaver, Rachel Cai, Chen Lin, Shuhan Cheng, Amy Culver, Yiyang Dong, Yao Gong, Guo Hongfei, Guo Xiyue, He Yining, Andrew Jin, Li Shu, Yurong Li, Gan Lin, Yu Chen Luo, Kaidi Lyu, Neil McCallum, Nyelin, Seth O'Farrell, Tong Pan, Yukun Peng, Sun Shulang, Camila Tay, Chenlin Wang, Wang Hanyu, Wang Luyu, Veronica Wong, Dan Wu, Wuyi, Xinyao, Claire Xiong, Hanhan Xu, Yan Jun, Zhang Bing, Zhang Heruijie, Rebecca Zhang, Christina Zhao.

Their linguistic talents have forged new paths for cultural exchange between China and the West, breaking barriers and fostering understanding through their contributions to Sino-British literature. As part of their contributions, they also brought cultural nuance to the text, including their thoughtful decisions on name order conventions. For the authors who used their original Chinese names, the names follow the original Chinese name order (family name before given name). For the translators, they have each chosen their preferred name order as some preserved the Chinese convention, while others adopted the convention of the West (given name before family name), showcasing the richness of cultural diversity. We deeply respect their choices and hope readers will appreciate this thoughtful approach.

Special thanks also go to the volunteer bilingual proofreaders of the English manuscript: Roseann Lake and Seth O'Farrell. Their mastery of both Chinese and English has provided the finishing touch to this work.

Finally, I express my deepest appreciation to Propolingo Publishing Ltd. for their steadfast support in bringing the English edition of this book to life. Thank you for walking with us in harmony, inspiring the world, amplifying the voices of the Chinese community, and creating yet another milestone in Sino-British cultural exchange.

With sincere gratitude and respect!

Xue Xinran
25 July, 2024